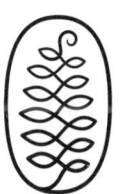

ADDITIONAL PRAISE FOR *PAPERS*

Papers, *one of the most extraordinary books I've ever read, is both a literary feat and an example of profound empathy. In their own words, we hear from the individuals whose stories are too often lost behind the vicious and inane labyrinth of the bureaucracies charged with handling "immigration policy." We are introduced to a kaleidoscope of peoples and experiences, their stories building up and out to reveal a broader landscape of pain, disappointment, humor, and kindness, ultimately portraying the grave realities of this system as well as the victories that are possible if, and only if, we refuse to accept institutional and governmental indifference and bigotry.*
NAFKOTE TAMIRAT, AUTHOR OF *THE PARKING LOT ATTENDANT*

Schwartz deftly isolates those moments when despair rises to the surface, as the years go by with no hope of a solution. The concrete lucidity of her prose allows us to feel all the more deeply the Kafkaesque absurdity of [the asylum-seekers'] situation. Without affectation, she plunges us into the heart of a system that has led to the creation of a parallel country, peopled by individuals reduced to numbers. SYLVIE TANETTE, *LES INROCKUPTIBLES*

Papers is a political work in the noblest sense of the term, a powerful and necessary text. SOPHIE JOUBERT, *L'HUMANITÉ*

So many life stories, conveyed here faithfully, that prove to be often captivating, sometimes appalling, always moving.
MARIANNE PAYOT, *L'EXPRESS*

Schwartz evokes the newspeak of French bureaucracy, from OQTF (mandatory expulsion from French territory) to RATATA (official denial of asylum). In counterpoint to this dehumanizing language are the raw spoken words of these "modern epics," accompanied here and there by a dose of caustic irony.
LAËTITIA GIANNECHINI, *LE MONDE DES LIVRES*

To be recognized by France's Ubuesque bureaucracy and escape deaths foretold, are they not often forced to fabricate proof of identity (that doesn't exist in their country) and sometimes, over endlessly repeated hearings, sensational fates to better connect with their interlocutors? Where has their truth gone? The author and musician works their language like a threnody, respectfully. If all these stories are alike, no two have the same sound, the same tone. These are the tragic epic poems of the present day, and the author lends them dignity and heroism through the quality of her writing.
FABIENNE PASCAUD, *TÉLÉRAMA*

PAPERS

Fern Books
Oakland, 94609
Paris, 75020
fernfernfern.com

Copyright © P.O.L Éditeur, 2019

Originally published in French as *Papiers*
by P.O.L Éditeur, 2019

First English edition, 2022
Translation copyright © Christine Gutman

All rights reserved. No part of this book may be reproduced, stored in a retrieval system, or transmitted in any form by any means, including mechanical, electronic, photocopy, recording, or otherwise, without the prior written consent of the publisher.

ISBN: 978-1-7352973-3-0 (paperback); 978-1-7352973-4-7 (ebook)
Library of Congress Control Number: 2022933286

Except where explicitly indicated, names, characters, places, and incidents in this book are used fictitiously.

Cover art and design by James David Lee
Interior design by Kit Schluter
Logo by Helen Shewolfe Tseng
Set in Cycles and Scala Sans

Printed in the United States

PAPERS

VIOLAINE SCHWARTZ

translated by Christine Gutman

FERN BOOKS
OAKLAND • PARIS

CONTENTS

Prologue	13
Glossary	19
Life Events, File No. 1409211219671	23
Dictation	39
Meanwhile…	40
Life Events, File No. 765893214677700007	41
Modern Languages	53
Of Hospitality	55
French History	61
Of Hospitality	63
Life Events, File No. 6648009421	71
Logic	83
Meanwhile…	84
Life Events, File No. 01126220022112	85
Mathematics	95
Life Events, File No. 45789999	96
Of Hospitality	107
Philosophy	120
Meanwhile…	121

Life Events, File No. 9878692438882	122
Meanwhile...	145
Composition	147
Of Hospitality	156
Meanwhile...	168
Acknowledgments	175

For Paul Otchakovsky-Laurens

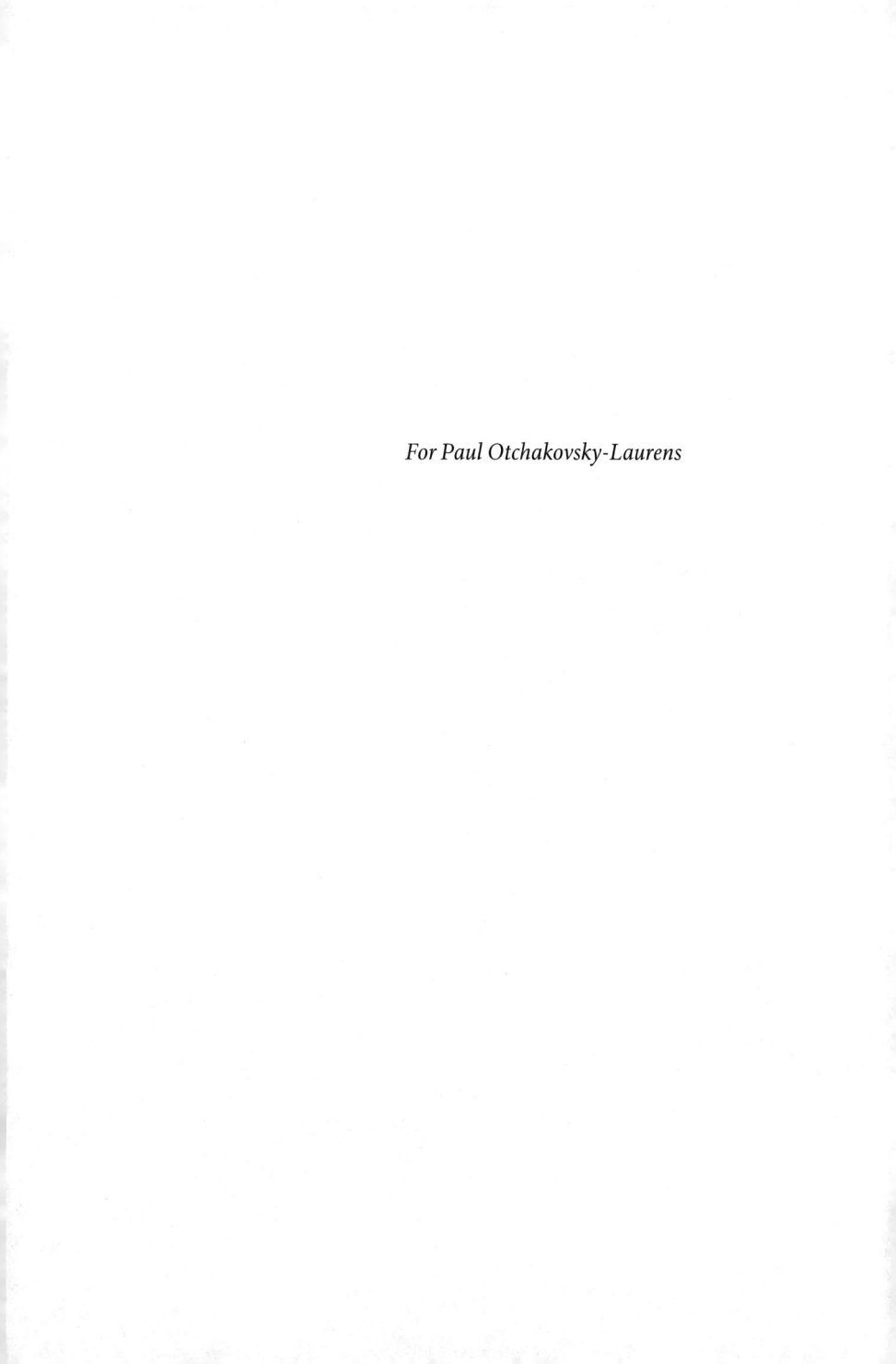

It started as a commission from the Centre Dramatique National in Besançon, France: to gather the oral histories of current and former asylum seekers and then write, using their words.
I had an office in the theater.
I had a tape recorder.
Sometimes I had an interpreter with me.
Pierre Couchot from the French Collective for the Defense of Foreigners' Rights and Liberties (CDDLE) volunteered to set up the appointments.
Over the course of a few days I met with ten people. Men, women, some young, some less so, all bound together by the same fate: the necessity to flee, to leave their native country behind. Afghanistan. Mauritania. Kosovo. Ethiopia. Armenia. Azerbaijan. Iraq.
Pierre Couchot also told me the stories of other people he had helped: people who had grown tired of telling the same story over and over. In vain. Tired of living on the edge of a precipice in France, with the same pain, an unhealing wound.
I was given photocopied biographical accounts, lists of documents, newspaper articles, photocopied minutes of immigration interviews,

administrative letters, rejection letters, petitions, memoranda from the Ministry of the Interior.
I met with a lawyer.
I attended hearings at the National Court of Asylum (CNDA) and the Besançon Administrative Court.
Then we learned that a family from Iraq had just arrived in Mouthe, a village in the mountainous Haut-Doubs region of eastern France with a population of 1,000 and a reputation as the coldest village in France.
A local association had been created to take them in.
I met the ten Iraqis and the members of the association.
I didn't write using the family's words directly, as the interviews took place in English. Doing so would have meant writing in a language I barely speak, and the constraint I had set myself was to write using the words I heard spoken: only those words.

To just listen.
To listen to those words and write them down.

Back home in Paris, I set out to meet the refugees living just outside my door, along the Canal Saint-Martin and under the arches of the elevated metro tracks between the Jaurès and La Chapelle stations.
I paid a visit to Français Langue d'Accueil, a language school for asylum seekers located in the 10th arrondissement.
I met the school's founders and a few more refugees — one of whom, upon reading my written version of his account, decided he preferred not to leave it in my hands. I had each person who spoke to me read

what I had written, which was perhaps crueler than a mirror. Or perhaps it brought to the surface a pain they would rather keep buried. Or perhaps the fear was still there—of their past catching up with them.

All these voices were in my computer, each one intoning a variation on the same theme: the absurdity of bureaucracy, the arbitrary workings of our justice system, the agony of waiting, the randomness of the journey, the pain of leaving everything behind, the courage to do so anyway, memories that still sting, survivor's guilt, lingering fear, but also hope, a new life forged in spite of it all, step by step on the path of exile, on the margins of our society.

Over and over, I listened to these stories.
These modern epics.
These heroic sagas.
I set them to the page.
To paper.

What struck me most was the need to speak.
To bear witness.
Words almost whispered.
Emotions held in check.
So that the voice might carry on.

There were sentences punctuated by eloquent errors.
Hands wrung with worry.

And always, slicing through every story, the vocabulary of French bureaucracy, barbed with acronyms.
A new language to decipher.
For them as for me.
Like school.
The school to which they are forced to return when they arrive here.
To start all over again.

GLOSSARY

ADA *(allocation pour demandeur d'asile)*
  welfare allowance for asylum seekers
AE *(arrêté d'expulsion)*
  deportation order
APMR *(arrêté préfectoral de maintien en rétention)*
  prefectural detention order
APRF *(arrêté préfectoral de reconduite à la frontière)*
  prefectural order to leave French territory
APS *(autorisation provisoire de séjour)*
  provisional residence permit
AR *(assignation à résidence)*
  house arrest
CADA *(centre d'accueil pour demandeurs d'asile)*
  housing and support center for asylum seekers
CNDA *(cour nationale du droit d'asile)*
  National Court of Asylum
CRA *(centre de rétention administrative)*
  administrative detention center

CR *(carte de résident)*
    residence permit
CST *(carte de séjour temporaire)*
    temporary residence permit
DA *(demandeur d'asile)*
    asylum seeker
DPAR *(dispositif de préparation au retour)*
    pre-departure housing facility for migrants denied asylum
FNE *(fichier national des étrangers)*
    national registry of foreigners
HUDA *(hébergement d'urgence des demandeurs d'asile)*
    emergency accommodation for asylum seekers
IRTF *(interdiction de retour sur le territoire français)*
    ban on re-entering French territory
LRA *(local de rétention administrative)*
    administrative detention site
MNA *(mineurs non accompagnés)*
    unaccompanied minors
NA *(non-admis)*
    asylum denied
OFII *(office français d'immigration et d'intégration)*
    French Office for Immigration and Integration
OFPRA *(office français de protection des réfugiés et apatrides)*
    French Office for the Protection of Refugees and Stateless Persons
OQTF *(obligation de quitter le territoire français)*
    mandatory expulsion from French territory

PAA *(procédure d'asile accélérée)*
   fast-track asylum procedure

PADA *(plateforme d'accueil des demandeurs d'asile)*
   reception platform for asylum seekers

PAF *(police aux frontières)*
   border police

RATATA *(refus d'admission sur le territoire au titre de l'asile)*
   official denial of asylum

UNESI *(unité nationale d'escorte, de soutien et d'intervention)*
   National Escort and Operational Support Tactical Unit

ZAPI *(zone d'attente pour personnes en instance)*
   pre-deportation airport detention facility

LIFE EVENTS, FILE NO. 1409211219671

Besançon?
That's just how it turned out.
By chance.
Go to Europe, figure it out, my ex-partner told me.
The father of my children, I mean.
I thought I would see him again one day, but no.
He gave me some money and then he left.
I figured it out as best I could.
Besançon.
It's a nice city.
I was lucky.
But the language is hard.
I didn't speak a word of French, I only knew how to say bonjour and maison.
I arrived with my two children on December 11, 2001, they were five and seven.
The driver dropped us on the side of the road.
You're in France, he told us, and then he left.
It was kind of him to take us that far.

If I'm not mistaken, now that I know the area, it was near Lyon.
We weren't dressed for December, it was cold.
I tried waving down cars to find out where I was.
In France, yes, but where?
Where?
We waited a long time in the winter wind and then a woman stopped.
Don't worry, she told me, we're somewhere.
She understood English.
I'm taking you to Besançon, you'll have to apply for asylum.
Driving over the bridge, I asked her the name of the river.
It's the Doo, she told me, and she pointed to a sign that said: DOUBS.
Why all those letters? You say Doo but you write all that?
She dropped us at the Secours Catholique.
They gave us coats there and called the PADA.
The reception platform for asylum seekers.
Back then it was in a barracks.
Why are you here, where are you from?
We're from Armenia.
How did you come?
Through Georgia. And then through Turkey.
How?
In a truck, hidden behind boxes. There were buckets in case the children had to do their business.
How many people were in the truck with you?
Just us.

Who was the driver?

I don't know his name.

So before we left my daughter had broken her arm, well, her arm was broken due to our problems, anyway, she had a cast, and all of a sudden in Istanbul it started bothering her, it was itching and she was crying, it had to come off, so I went to the red market in the Armenian neighborhood to get help because I didn't speak Turkish and I found an Armenian who told me: I will help you.

He's the one who found the truck driver, the smugglers, he took care of everything. I was not in a mental state to do it, but I did have money.

How much did you pay for the trip?

It's gone from my memory but I had enough.

What were your reasons for leaving?

We have to go all the way back to the beginning.

Otherwise it makes no sense.

So.

So.

Where to begin?

I was apparently born on March 8, 1975 in Masis, Armenia.

I say apparently because I have no birth certificate.

I have nothing.

Nothing at all.

Only my word.

All I know is we always celebrated my birthday on March 8.

I remember because it's International Women's Day.

And I also know my parents were born in Azerbaijan, they're Azeri.

Back then,

I mean in the days of the USSR,

there was no conflict between Armenia and Azerbaijan,

there were even intermarriages.

I think they came to Armenia to have me.

There was a good gynecologist there back then who treated my mother and it worked, I was born.

After that, they stayed there.

Everyone liked us in the village.

Until the Nagorno–Karabakh conflict, in 1988.

Then it became like a war.

And then there was the Sumgait pogrom.

And after that, in Armenia, Azeris became like traitors.

They were persecuted.

Beaten.

Killed.

They called us Turks, in reference to the Armenian genocide.

They still do today.

Filthy Turks! Filthy Turks!

My parents decided to go back to Azerbaijan.

It was becoming too dangerous.

Our bags were packed.

I went to school to say goodbye to my friends.

I was thirteen.

And on the way home,
on the way,
on the,
a neighbor grabbed me by the hand,
she lived three houses up from ours,
and she threw me in her cellar.
You have to stay here, she told me, that's all she said.
I had no idea what was happening, I just sat there crying all alone in the dark.
Only when night fell did she come back down to see me and that was when she told me,
I don't remember exactly how,
but she told me:
Some people burned your house down, you don't have a house anymore and you don't have parents anymore either, they killed your parents.
That's all she told me.
I stayed hidden in the cellar for three days.
At night, she would bring food down to me, without making a sound, she was nice, she was just afraid of getting caught.
So it occurred to her to leave me with Rima.
Rima was a woman who lived in Yerevan, the capital of Armenia.
She had no children, she was a schoolteacher.
She agreed to adopt me,
"adopt" me,

because there were no papers, nothing.
No written trace.
Just her word.
But I had no choice.
There was emptiness all around me.
I just wanted to join my parents in death,
I did whatever I was told.
The OFPRA asked me why I didn't go back to Azerbaijan.
It's true.
It hadn't even occurred to me.
I had family there.
My mother's parents?
Or my father's?
I don't know.
I never met them.
They were strangers to me.
And I was scared.
And I didn't speak their language very well. I went to an Armenian school.
So I ended up with Rima.
With Rima I was homeschooled, because I couldn't go out, I had no papers, it was war every day and I had Azeri blood in my veins.
Forget all that, Rima told me.
Erase that word from your head.
Azeri.

It's over.

We'll say you're Armenian, we'll say your parents went to Russia to work, we'll say I'm watching you, you'll go out as little as possible.

There was a big library in her apartment.

I just read all day long.

Read and learned.

I had nothing else to do.

Except sometimes when we went to see her cousin, he was my age.

But that wasn't very often.

It was the books that held me up.

It was the books that saved me.

Rima was single, she was happy to have me around, we got along well.

She didn't replace the emptiness but we got along well.

She explained to me that not everyone in the country wanted to kill me.

Not all of them.

Because every night I thought:

Will it happen again?

Like in the village?

Like that day?

I went home, there was nothing left.

No house.

No one.

Nothing.

I have no photos.

I have nothing.

Nothing left of my parents.

Sometimes I try to dream to see if I remember their faces.

I don't.

I see different faces every time.

I'm your mother, I'm your father, they say in my ear, but how do I know?

I've lost the key to knowing where I come from.

It burned with everything else.

But you have to keep going.

Where was I?

Rima.

She had a heart attack and she died all at once. I was eighteen.

I couldn't stay at her place, it was a government apartment.

I didn't know what to do with myself, all over again.

So I went to see her cousin.

Let's live together, he told me, after all we love each other.

He was Armenian. I told him the truth.

We can't get married, I have no papers, I have no parents in Russia, there's no one to ask for my hand, no one, I told him.

I had to tell him.

Anyway, I had nothing to lose.

Nothing.

I had already lost everything.

At first he just stood there, stunned.

He couldn't believe I was Azeri, I spoke better Armenian than he did, I'd studied the literature and everything.
And then there was the issue of his parents.
Because he was in love, yes, but then there was his parents.
They were dentists.
They wanted absolutely no part in any of this, they were scared.
They bought us an apartment, they were very kind, but they didn't want to see much of us.
I understand.
I was scared too.
I went out as little as possible.
I was always afraid that someone would recognize me.
Someone from my village.
Armenia isn't very big.
I learned chemistry, for five years, between my four walls.
They had a cousin who desperately wanted a degree in chemistry but she wasn't a very good student, she was always partying.
I learned chemistry for her. I took the exams for her.
And I passed.
I have a degree in chemistry but it's not in my name.
It's like my children. Their births were never registered.
Since I had no papers, I couldn't go to the hospital.
I gave birth at home, in secret.
You can't live your whole life in secret.
You can't live your whole life saying your purse just got stolen.
We tried to buy papers.

Back then in Armenia you could.

My former in-laws spent a lot of money, but in the end nothing came of it.

The problem came with the national census.

All of a sudden we had to register.

And this time it was national, the purse story wouldn't do.

My ex gave his passport.

Your papers, ma'am?

Ma'am, your papers, please.

Your papers.

Do you understand?

Your papers.

She's registered in Masis, my ex told them.

That's the name of the village where I was apparently born.

I say apparently because there's no trace of me there.

Nowhere.

Last year I hired a lawyer to find a birth certificate in my name.

But there's nothing in Masis in your name, she told me.

She searched all over Armenia,

she left no stone unturned,

there is no trace of you anywhere, she told me.

There is no trace of me anywhere.

And yet here I am, right?

And yet I exist physically.

Sometimes I wonder.

Sometimes I pinch myself to be sure I'm really here.

Ouch!

And so.
So, where was I?
She's registered in Masis, my ex told the cops.
He didn't mean to, it just came out, in the panic.
Very well, we'll be back in two weeks.
They looked into it and discovered that in 1988 an Azeri family was killed in Masis but that the third person went missing and so that was me.
They came back just like they said and they started beating us.
Telling my ex he was a traitor.
Telling me:
Get lost, filthy Muslim, you don't have the right to live here.
And then they came back again.
Once.
Twice.
They destroyed everything in my ex's shop.
Mirrors in a thousand pieces.
They threw my daughter against the wall.
So. It wasn't easy.
We had to leave.
We had to leave as fast as we could.
But the problem was, I couldn't walk.
I was dizzy all the time.
Because they had hit me so much on the head.
My former in-laws found someone who would take me in, in a village far from the capital.
I was on a ton of medications.

By December I was doing a little better.

Now figure it out, my ex told me.

You're a big girl. You have to get out of here.

I've had it. I've lost everything because of you, everything.

His cars, his shop, his apartment, everything.

He was an only child, spoiled by his parents, and now all of a sudden he had to go hide out in the country like a criminal.

He was mad, I understand that.

It doesn't matter, it's over.

After my parents, nothing matters.

He said goodbye to us at the border and I made it to Besançon.

I thought I would see him again one day, but no.

He turned his back.

I applied for asylum at the OFPRA.

I was rejected.

For lack of proof.

They wanted proof that I was actually Azeri and that the name I gave was my real name, but I had nothing.

No papers.

Only my word.

The day your parents died, why didn't you go back for your ID?

But the house had burned down.

Why didn't you go to the town hall?

At thirteen, it didn't occur to me.

Today, if there was a problem, the first thing I'd take would be my papers. But at thirteen the only thing I wanted was to die.

How could I prove that I had been beaten nearly to death?

Pardon me, officer, could you please sign this statement for me?
I didn't have a medical report either.
No doctor would have signed a report for an Azeri.
They treated me at night, in secret, in exchange for a lot of money.
I filed an appeal with the CNDA.
Well, the social workers did it for me.
I was in the hospital for depression, I'd stopped eating, I weighed eighty-four pounds.
But again.
We need proof.
We need proof.
The process took five years in all.
From my initial application for asylum to the appeal.
Five years of waiting.
For a yes or a no.
And at the end, we were rejected.
Since I was still in the hospital, the social workers petitioned the district to grant me a special residence permit for sick foreigners.
And in May 2005,
finally some good news:
I got my first residence permit, good for one year.
But I was still in the hospital.
Novillars Hospital.
My children were at a crisis shelter.

They can't stay there forever, they'll have to be placed with a foster family, the social worker told me, you're not able to take care of them.

And that, that was what I needed to hear.

I decided to pull through.

For them.

I chose to get better.

I asked the doctor to let me have custody of them,

every day,

every day,

every day.

And finally they gave me a trial period of one week, to see how it went.

It went well.

I was getting my strength back.

Little by little.

I started eating again.

Little by little.

And I managed to get out of the hospital.

I found an apartment downtown.

But I was scared of everything.

If someone raised their voice near me, I would burst into tears.

One morning I decided the only way to get better was by working.

Like when I lived with Rima.

Working, learning.

Books, books.

But I had no degree here. Not even a high school diploma.

There are jobs in home care, the job coach told me, or in retail.

I said, I don't care, I just want to work.

The unemployment office offered me a position as a special needs assistant for handicapped children. For five years I worked in primary schools.

It got me back on my feet.

In 2011, I got a permanent position as an in-home caregiver.

I take care of an autistic child, he was too violent for the facilities.

I have scars all over, but I managed to form a bond with him.

I've taught him to read and count and write.

I work with autism specialists in Switzerland.

Soon I will take my exams.

If I pass all the modules, I'll finally have a degree in my name.

Little by little, I'm coming back to life.

My children just got French citizenship.

And I have a ten-year residence permit.

I changed my status from sick foreigner to care worker.

It's valid through 2020.

I have another three years ahead of me.

On the permit it says:

Country: unspecified.

Nationality: unspecified.

In stores I never pay by check, because you have to show an ID and when people see nationality unspecified, they look at me funny.

Unspecified, what's that?

It's me.

The lawyer can't find me anywhere.

She searched all over Armenia, there's no trace of me.

Nowhere.

So was I really born there?

I wonder.

Were my parents my real parents?

I wonder.

They had trouble having a child.

Maybe they adopted me and never told me?

In Armenia, you wait until your child is grown to tell that kind of truth.

So maybe I am an Armenian after all?

But in that case, then who are my real parents?

There are always whys in my head.

Maybe I don't exist.

I wonder.

There's no proof of me.

Nowhere.

DICTATION

The passport is the noblest part of a human being period
Moreover comma a passport is not as easy to make as a human being period
A human being can be made anywhere comma in the most impulsive of ways and with no sound reason semicolon
A passport comma never period
Therefore comma we recognize the value of a good passport comma
Whereas a human being comma however good comma
Will not necessarily be recognized period

By Bertolt Brecht spelled as it sounds

MEANWHILE...

The wild geese

fly   *free*

   fly   *free*

     fly   *free*

       fly   *free*

         fly   *free*

           fly   *free*

             fly   *free*

               flee

LIFE EVENTS, FILE NO. 765893214677700007

My first name is Habibullah and my last name is Amini.
I arrived in Paris on May 25, 2015.
I have been here for over two years.
I met people on the road who told me:
We're going to Paris.
Can I come with you?
I wanted to go to France but I didn't know where exactly.
It was best to go with them.
With friends.
First I went to Iran. I stayed there for six months.
Then I went to Turkey.
Then to Greece. I took a boat to a little island called Kos and then I took a bigger boat to Athens.
From there I continued by foot, by car, by train, by bus, by any way possible.
The smugglers told us how to do it.
I passed through Macedonia, Serbia, Austria, Hungary, Germany, and finally I got to France.
But I stayed for a long time in Turkey and Iran.

To pay for the journey.

I didn't have any money because I had to leave Kabul very fast after prison.

In Tehran I worked in a factory that makes plastic containers.

I didn't have legal residency there, I went out once a week, slept in the factory, gave my boss money for food.

In Turkey, in Istanbul, I worked in a bakery, I made bread and Turkish croissants.

In Greece, in the province of Argos, I worked in a garden picking oranges.

I was in prison because I used to be a driver, a minibus driver.

I worked the route between Parwan and Kabul.

The day I was arrested,

that day,

I was driving some people I didn't know.

Villagers.

We were searched at a checkpoint.

The villagers had a lot of bags.

I thought it was food, but inside, hidden among the beans, the police found parts of weapons, Kalashnikovs, things like that, things to make war.

Every year, in my country, there is a war between the nomads and the villagers.

We say nomads, but in truth they are Taliban.

They are Taliban disguised as nomads, they come with sheep, but in truth they have weapons.

Every year these Taliban disguised as nomads try to drive the villagers from their homes.

This land, it's ours, all of it.

The villagers say they have lived there for fifteen, twenty generations.

Who says this land is yours? It's ours.

Every year it happens again.

The villagers are ethnic Hazaras, like me.

The nomads are Pashtuns, they come in the summer, they kill people, they make war, and when it gets too cold they leave, they go away, and the next summer they come back and every year it happens again.

That day the villagers told the police the bags were mine, but it wasn't true.

So the police put us in prison. All of us together.

The villagers and me.

I didn't know them, I had never seen them before, that is the truth.

We were locked in one big room and the villagers kept telling me:

The sacks of food are yours. Say it. They're yours. Got it? If you ever say they're ours we will kill your whole family.

A month later the villagers were released, and I stayed in prison.

It's because they paid.

In Afghanistan, for a baksheesh, anything is possible.

I am the oldest son of the family. My father was a general. He was killed.

I have no one to help me.

I have no one to defend me.

I have a brother but he is too young.

So I was all alone that day.

That's why I stayed in prison.

My lawyer told me:

The villagers aren't guilty because the van belonged to you.

But it's not good to turn your back on the truth, I drove them, that's all. I don't look inside sacks of flour. Or sacks of beans. I drive, that's all.

No one believed me because I didn't have money to pay the judge.

My lawyer back there wasn't like the ones in France.

He wasn't there to defend me, he just said he was.

In truth, he had received money in secret from the villagers.

I spent three months in prison.

One day, my mother came to visit, in tears:

Some villagers came to see me last night. You have to say the bags were yours, do you hear me? Yours. If you don't, they're going to come back and kill us. Do you hear? Yours.

I said the bags were mine.

What else could I do?

But after that I was very scared.

Of being hanged by the government.

Of spending years in prison.

That's when I thought of someone I sort of knew who worked for the police in Kabul.

I talked to my mother about it.

She sold all her jewelry, everything we had of value in the house, to get money, and she gave it all to him.

And he paid off one of the prison guards to let me leave with the families at the end of visiting hours.

In the prison there are only three or four guards watching the inmates, it's more like a little jail.

There are daytime guards and nighttime guards.

That day, the daytime guard brought me over to the family side and I walked out.

My brother and a friend were waiting with a car, they drove me very fast to Maidan Wardak, and then I took a taxi so I could get to Nimroz, a city on the Iranian border, before midnight.

I had to leave Afghanistan before the nighttime guards went on duty.

By the time I got to Nimroz the nighttime guards already knew I had escaped.

So they went to see my mother:

Where is Habibullah?

He's in your prison, she told them, I saw him there yesterday.

Even today she is still harassed.

They come to see her and they ask her:

Where is Habibullah?

Police, men, women, villagers.

My mother always replies:
I don't know. He was in prison. Maybe you killed him?
My mother has to keep moving from place to place.
Sometimes she lives here and sometimes there.
The situation is terrorful in Afghanistan.
Sorry, I mean terrible.
Why?
Because you're Hazara.
Why?
Because you're Shiite.
Why?
Because you're honest.
We're not guilty. We don't make war.
That is why they kill us.
For the last few hundred years they have killed us for no reason.
Women, children.
If you have an Asian face, they arrest you, they kill you for no reason.
Like me.
They say we aren't Afghans. That we aren't Muslims. That we are refugees. Because we come from Mongolia.
Who says that?
The Taliban. The Pashtuns.
That is why I have to live here, far from my family.
I had to leave everything behind.
I had to start over, from nothing.
The day I arrived in Paris,

that day,

right away I looked for the Gare de l'Est train station because, on the way here, I had heard about a place with lots of Afghans called the Gare de l'Est.

Back home everybody knows about the park by the Gare de l'Est.

It's more famous than the Eiffel Tower.

I talked to people there and little by little I found some friends.

I found out how I could take a shower, how I could get something to eat.

I slept on the street for six months.

It was almost summer but still, it was hard.

I couldn't wait to apply for asylum in France.

I went to France Terre d'Asile, I stood in line and I got an appointment for twenty days later.

And then I thought: I have to learn French, very fast.

I bought a notebook and a pen to learn in the streets.

I asked people walking by, in English:

Hello, how can I say hello in French?

How do I say goodbye?

Then I found out about Emmaus, but there was no room for me.

I waited for five months.

One day I had an argument with the volunteer in charge of the new people and I ripped up my card.

I'm not coming anymore, it's taking too long.

Two weeks later he called me.

That's how I got a spot in a French class.

Now I'm working hard to speak the language well.

To take the exam.

And I'm waiting to hear about my papers.

This is my second time applying.

Because of the Hungary problem.

Because I had to leave my fingers there.

I told them I didn't want to stay in Hungary, that I wanted to go to France, but they put me in prison for a day and a night, they made me give my fingerprints and then they let me go.

You can leave! Now we know the French government will send you back here!

And that's what happened, just like they said.

When I got to Paris, I went to the main Prefecture.

You're not allowed to apply for asylum in France. You have to wait at least ten months, until your procedure with Hungary expires.

I had been Dublin Procedured.

Dublined to Hungary.

One day I received a deportation order.

I had to turn myself in at the Prefecture to be sent back to Hungary.

That day, I went into hiding.

For ten months I stayed in hiding.

I had to avoid getting arrested at all costs, or else it was back to Hungary.

I waited for the ten months to pass and then I went back to the Prefecture and that day, it worked.

That day, they took my prints and they gave me the story notebook.

That's what we all call it.

The notebook to write your story in.

To explain why you came.

The notebook you have to send to the OFPRA.

I had my interview on August 26, 2016.

It's already been over a year.

Everything went well, the lady said she would send me the response three weeks later, but I still haven't received anything.

I can wait.

I have time to learn French.

To get to know French society.

I know very well that one day I'll get the response.

If they want the truth, I'll be okay.

If not, I don't know.

You have to at least try.

I just want to be independent in France.

Right now, we are totally dependent on the French government for housing, for money, for everything.

How many refugees are there in France?

The government pays 330 euros per person.

What does that add up to?

That's why I want to be independent.

To pay taxes. To give back to the French government. To pay for all the things I've been given here.

Right now I'm not allowed to work, but I volunteer at Emmaus.

That community, they are my family.
I live in Montparnasse with a very kind lady.
She's like my adoptive mother.
She houses me, she gives me French lessons.
The first most important thing in life is language.
I've learned French thanks to volunteers.
And I try to help others too.
I help the people who don't speak well.
The paperwork, you don't understand any of it when you first arrive.
Everything I've learned I share with the others.
I go see the Afghans, my friends.
Every day I go around to all my places.
The Gare de l'Est is very hard, I know that.
When I first arrived, I slept on a cardboard box.
Between you and me, sometimes it was okay and sometimes it wasn't, it's different for everybody.
We come from different provinces.
We speak different languages.
Your brain doesn't work right when it's too hard outside.
All the time you're angry.
At yourself, too, and that's the worst.
I've tried to cross over to the other side, to learn the language, to get to know Paris, to have French friends, but the others, they keep to themselves, they play cards and soccer with each other.
Currently in Paris there are lots of Pakistanis.

They cheat.
They get identity cards from Afghanistan.
They cheat.
They show Afghan driver's licenses.
They cheat.
They'll get asylum.
But you have to tell the truth.
These days in France the real Afghans get a rejection and the Pakistanis get asylum.
These days it's hard for Afghans because last year our president came to Germany,
and he signed an agreement with the European countries that said:
You can send all Afghans back to Afghanistan, except the Pashtuns.
And that's what is happening right now in France, in Germany.
For the Pashtuns: asylum.
For the other ethnicities: rejection.
These days in Afghanistan they stab you in the back, with a pen.
That is the truth.
From behind, they strike with a pen.
Before, Afghanistan was called Ariana.
That means: the country for everyone, for all ethnicities.
But one day a king decided to change the name of the country.
He called his country Afghanistan. That means: Pashtuns.
Afghan means Pashtun.

It is a country only for Pashtuns.

The Hazaras, either they go to Mongolia or they go to the cemetery.

That is why I left that day.

That is why I am here today.

MODERN LANGUAGES

Translate the verb *to hope* into

Albanian.
Arabic.
Syriac.
Berber.
Farsi.
Pashto.
Armenian.
Fula.
Wolof.

Translate the verb *to reject* into

German.
French.
Hungarian.
Spanish.
Swedish.
Greek.
Italian.
Swiss.
Belgian.

OF HOSPITALITY
The Language School No. 1

I used to walk through the Jardin Villemin every day but I never saw them.
It's funny sometimes how we're blind.
We walk right by, maybe we're lost in thought.
My kids were growing up. I didn't see them.
They were all strewn across one part of the park,
always the same part,
almost like flowers.
And all of a sudden,
I saw them and I felt guilty.
I could understand what they were saying because I speak Dari.
Dari and Farsi, they're almost the same.
I wanted to do something.
I talked about it with the parishioners at Église Saint-Laurent.
We decided to host a breakfast every Saturday.
I would go get them in the park:
Come on, it's cold out here, come with me.
I was the only one in the church group who could talk to them.

It ended up being a big success.

Little by little, from sixty people, we got to two hundred and they would all line up and wait, like anywhere in Paris — the bank, the post office.

That wasn't the warm welcome we were going for.

So after six months, we stopped the experiment.

It was too difficult.

But it kept nagging at me, so I decided to organize some French classes.

Is there anybody who would be interested? Let's go see the priest, he must have some rooms available.

When do you want to start? he asked me.

Right away.

And so he gave me the keys to a space on Rue Philippe-de-Girard where we're still teaching today.

I went to get the Afghans in the park but they were quite wary.

Who knows where this crazy lady wants to take us.

Eventually a small group came along and so we got started, every Saturday.

But it quickly became clear that it wasn't enough.

We asked the priest if we could have Wednesdays as well.

And then we realized that two days wouldn't do either.

So it ended up being six days a week.

There were five or six teachers in all.

We had tons of ideas:

Bring in benches.

Find some pens.

We got supplies at secondhand stores.
It was exciting.
These were our first classes.
We were quite close to those first students.
We saw them quite often.
We grew together through the challenges.
There was a group of serious students, journalists who were used to learning and who wanted to go fast, but there were also a lot of people who were learning to read and sleeping in the streets.
One day Christian said:
We should register as an association, so we're covered if there's a problem.
But we were still basically operating out of the church.
I went to see the priest.
He said that as far as he was concerned it wasn't a pastoral activity.
That was fine with us.
We wanted it to be secular.
The association was founded in March 2010.
At first we didn't have an office.
It was virtual.
Then we found a small space in Belleville for close to nothing.
We got funding to hire an educational coordinator.
But pretty soon we were packed in like sardines, with more and more students.
We looked for a bigger space.

And last January we moved here, 28 Rue de l'Aqueduc, in the 10th arrondissement.

Our classes are exclusively for non-French-speaking asylum seekers.

It started with the Afghans but it's not just for them.

We offer language instruction, professional integration assistance, and cultural and athletic activities.

We also help them prepare their stories for the OFPRA.

If it's too complicated, if a lawyer's help is required, we send them to the GISTI.

That's the information and support group for refugees.

We started out with fifty students.

Now we have over seven hundred.

Say there were a natural disaster, an earthquake

— I mean it's not like that's going to happen in Paris, but let's just imagine —

the government would convert vacant lots and abandoned buildings, they would make it work,

but in this case they do nothing.

They're afraid of opening the floodgates.

If we help them, then they'll all start coming.

But before we start worrying about them flooding in,

and flooding in,

and flooding in,

we have to take care of the ones who are already here.

The ones sleeping on the ground.

If they can get out of that situation,
I tell myself,
if they can pick up a little bit of French,
if they can meet their basic needs,
that's a good start.
But we have to accept that we can't fix everything.
In the beginning, those first two years, I had nightmares.
How could they have been through all that?
How can you not let it get to you?
You'd have to be like a doctor.
The other day I learned an Iranian expression that means "to see pain."
That's exactly what it is.
You have to learn to see pain.
We have this one student, a photographer, twenty years old, who got arrested.
He tried to kill himself three times because his situation in Afghanistan was hopeless,
he knew he'd be killed if he got sent back.
Like so many others.
Luckily, there was a technicality.
We managed to get him released from the detention center.
Another one I knew nearly lost his mind.
He was older, fortysomething.
The police brought him to the airport, strapped into a wheelchair.

It was barbaric — blindfolded, gagged so he couldn't scream.
I don't know how he got out of that situation but it drove him insane.
They couldn't get him on the plane, so they put him in a mental hospital.
I went to see him there.
Little by little things settled down and he was released.
I haven't heard from him since.
I guess he must have gotten his papers.
Then there was another one who went back home on his own initiative.
He had stopped hearing from his wife, his children, he was convinced they were in danger, he was so close to getting his papers, getting through the whole ordeal, but he decided to go back to his country to protect his family.
Then there are those who want to cut all ties to their past.
And you think of the children waiting for their father, he's going to come back, he's going to call.
And those who died in the mountains or at sea.
Who saw people die right beside them.
So, yes, I have lots of stories in my head.
That's what we're here for too.
To listen.
It's so important that we have this office,
our home base here on the Rue de l'Aqueduc.
If anybody wants to check in, they know we're here.

FRENCH HISTORY

Fill in the blank with the correct ethnic or tribal denomination(s) from the choices below.

Our ancestors the _____.

Celts
  Osismii
        Coriosolites
        Veneti
   Aulerci Cenomani
   Parisii
       Volcae Tectosages
        Volcae Arecomici
   Allobroges
         Senones
       Boii
    Arverni Helvetii

       Romans

                Visigoths
                        Goths
                                        Ostrogoths

                Vandals
Burgundians
                                        Aquitanians
                                                Ausci
                        Lactorates
                Garumni
                        Cocosates
        Convenae

                        Ligurians
                                                Vocontii
                                        Franks
                                                Huns
                                Suebi

                                Saxons   Alemanni

                        Laeti   Vikings

                                Alans

OF HOSPITALITY
The Language School No. 2

I've lived in this neighborhood for over thirty years.
I saw the first tents go up along the canal when they closed the camp in Sangatte.
The first spillover from Calais to Paris.
They came through the Gare du Nord.
And it's not like there are tons of spots to settle around here.
There's the Square Alban-Satragne and the Jardin Villemin.
I saw these people outside, right in front of my building.
I looked up community associations to try to do something.
I found the Exilé 10 collective but I didn't fit in there.
I contacted France Terre d'Asile but my inquiry got lost in a maze of red tape.
And then, in early 2009, I heard about the French classes.
I called Chantal and she told me to stop by the space on Rue Philippe-de-Girard.
When I got there, Marysia said to me:
Here's a small group, they're all yours.
Okay then, here goes nothing.

I teach at a university, so it wasn't like she was throwing me into the lions' den, but still, it was a little strange, especially in that tiny space.

At first I took it slow, once or twice a week.

And then we were getting a lot of new students, so I took charge of things, I was on sabbatical.

In early 2010 the writer Atiq Rahimi was interviewed on France Culture and he mentioned us:

There are these good people giving French classes to Afghans in the 10th.

And France Culture shared my email address with listeners.

I got tons of messages of support.

I offered to set up a formal association.

We had a classroom.

We had volunteers.

Everything was in place.

When we first started out there were four hundred Afghans seeking asylum in France.

Now, in 2017, there are over six thousand.

No big deal, just fifteen times more.

One problem with the way the government handles it is this idea that if you make them suffer long enough they'll give up and go home.

That's not how it works.

They stay.

They've gone through so much to get here that they're staying.

Our policy makes no sense.

It destroys people and they stay anyway.
But now they aren't contributing what they could contribute.
These people are healthy overall, and very resourceful.
After a few years of being treated this way, they've lost everything.
They've lost their health, their money, and they've gotten so used to dropping it all and starting over that they just can't recover.
A lot of them suffer from depression.
The reality they find when they get here,
they don't tell their families about it.
They're disillusioned by the way the authorities treat them, and with good reason.
They go half mad from waiting.
Realizing you've been cheated, that's got to be painful.
But they don't tell their families about it.
And even if they do, no one back home believes them.
A lot of them are married and have children already.
They have kids very young, at twenty.
And as hard as their life is, they still think they're going to bring the kids here.
Except for a few who've moved on.
They've waited in Europe for too long, they've done ten years in Europe, trying to get a foothold in Europe.
After ten years, your kids, your wife ...
Your life is in pieces.
It's the "middle" class who comes here.

It's not the poorest ones, they go next door to Iran.

It's not the richest ones, they go to Dubai, places like that.

It's the ones who are healthy and who can afford the trip.

I know one who told his parents:

Whatever you do, don't come here. At your age, your life will be as good as over.

His parents ended up listening to him, even though they could afford the trip, and six months later they go to the capital of their province, they get arrested at a Taliban roadblock, and the father gets kidnapped.

They let him go and it wasn't too expensive, they were lucky, but then they took the uncle, and that time they didn't let him go.

And then you have the opposite scenario: this one woman told her family to leave and her nephew and brother-in-law ended up dying in the mountains in Kurdistan.

So there's no right choice.

When I hear other people here doling out advice, I say: Don't.

It's like this whole idea of the good immigrant, the political refugee, versus the economic migrant.

As Français Langue d'Accueil volunteers, we don't want to get involved.

We don't bear judgment.

That's one of the founding principles of the association, in fact.

We take them as they come, regardless of whatever problem brought them here.

And you know, it's never straightforward.

There's always a gray area.

Say there's an Afghan who's lived for years as a refugee in Iran.

He gets sent back to his country but he doesn't know anyone there anymore.

So what does he do?

He leaves again, but not for Iran, since they just kicked him out.

He goes to Europe.

You might say it's political, since he got deported from Iran because of his nationality.

But there might be other factors at play too.

Let's say, oh, I don't know:

His father beat him and he was no longer accustomed to being beaten by his father.

Or his father hit his mother and this time he stepped in and things got ugly.

Maybe he made some incidental mistake because he was no longer used to life in Afghanistan,

and now someone jumps on that to make trouble for his family.

What type of departure is that?

Political?

Economic?

Familial?

We prefer to stay out of it.

Besides, if there's one thing I've learned over the years, it's that the truth is always a far cry from what you think.

I don't want to meddle in the story they tell themselves.
Because you need a believable story for the OFPRA, and for that you have to make adjustments, it's practically a necessity, and you have to convince yourself, and everyone you talk to, that those adjustments are true.
We all have our secrets.
But this is for the courts. This is for papers.
Sometimes they come up with stories that are a lot less believable than what they actually experienced.
Because there are things they think they can't say.
If they're gay, for instance.
Or stories involving drugs.
Kids who've been forced into trafficking, against their will.
They think you can't say that here.
So they go see the story peddlers.
There really is such a thing.
Story peddlers.
I come from such-and-such region. What do I say?
It costs about a hundred euros.
Written in atrocious French.
So bad that the names change throughout the story.
Mohammed Kachi becomes Ahmed Kachi and then Ahmed Something Else Entirely.
I've actually had to tell someone:
Change your story, it just doesn't hold up.
There's also the age issue.
For the younger ones it's a huge deal.

They choose based on their physical appearance.

Many Afghans don't have a birth certificate.

That's why, on their papers in France, most of them were born on January 1.

Occasionally, at the whim of the immigration agent, they were born on the 3rd or the 5th, for variety.

And that can lead to the absurd scenario of a kid who genuinely doesn't know how old he is.

If they're registered as minors, they can't be deported.

It's better that way.

The ones under sixteen can go to school, they put them in a special-needs class, that way they chalk up more time here — it's worth it.

But over sixteen, there's not much to be gained.

They just let you wait patiently until you turn eighteen and that's that.

Because applying for asylum means applying to wait, and that way they're just adding another year to that wait, so...

On a similar note, a lot of Afghans don't have a last name.

They just have a first name.

They make up a last name when they get to Europe.

The Pashtuns take the name of their tribe, their clan.

All -khel names, those are Pashtun clan names.

The Number Two Afghan executive, after the president, is named Abdullah Abdullah.

He took a last name just to humor journalists, and it's not like he comes from some peasant family way up in the mountains.

Now they're in the process of setting up a registration system in Afghanistan, but that's going to take time.

And so, when you ask them the question What is your last name? it's understandable if they get it wrong, because most of the time it has no meaning for them.

For us, it's self-evident, it's our identity, but for them, right from the beginning, they're stuck.

The last name doesn't compute.

The date of birth doesn't either.

Which is how our legal system has created a parallel system of organized lies.

LIFE EVENTS, FILE NO. 6648009421

I am Mrs. Cissé, that is the name of my late husband who passed away.
I kept his last name. My first name is Djoubo (see birth certificate).
I arrived in Besançon in 2005 with my husband to apply for asylum.
We couldn't stay in Mauritania any longer because of the white Moors who are racist like you cannot imagine.
In 1989 they took power and they arrested all the blacks.
All the people like us.
Civil servants, soldiers, coast guards, police officers, customs officers.
They arrested all the blacks in the Mauritanian government (see attached press clippings)
and they killed, killed, killed.
It was the infamous denegrification of the Mauritanian government.
If you don't want problems, get rid of all the blacks, Saddam Hussein said.

My husband Mr. Cissé was a customs officer.

He was chief customs officer.

When he left for work I never knew if he would come back.

One day your husband gets a summons from the head white Moor and it's all over, you never see him again and that's that.

Some were deported to Senegal.

Some were thrown into a dumpster, like sacks of rice.

My sister's husband, he was thrown into a dumpster.

One cursed morning, they summoned my husband.

This was in August of 1990.

They summoned Cissé, a friend of Cissé's told me.

I was all in a tizzy.

I was up and I was down all at once.

I started running around everywhere.

And crying and crying.

Inshallah.

And I was with child too.

Stay calm, Cissé's friend told me. Stay calm, I'll get him out of this.

And he did as he said, Cissé's friend.

Ten days later, at two in the morning, he came for me.

Hurry, hurry, cover yourself, I'm taking you to my garage in Nouadhibou.

I put on a traditional dress with a headscarf and I got into his car.

Vroom.

All the way to the garage.

Later on, another car came in the night.

Vrooom.

And inside, there was Cissé.

He was covered in blood, he was naked, but he was alive.

He told me: I'm okay.

Even if we're not okay, he and I, we always say we're okay.

Okay.

Always okay.

He was wounded all over.

Like a slave.

We started crying.

No, no, now is not the time, Cissé's friend said. We'll see what we can do. But you can't stay in the garage, you're going to go home and you're not going to tell anyone that Cissé is hiding here, not even your sister, and you'll come see him every ten days in your veiled dress and that's that.

Okay.

That's what we did.

Every ten days I would go to Nouadhibou, hidden under my headscarf.

Until February of 1991, when they liberated Kuwait.

Saddam Hussein left Kuwait and right away, at five in the morning, the white Moors started letting out black prisoners.

Blessed morning!

Cissé could come home.

No more garage.

Cissé's friend left him in my bedroom.

Everywhere there were husbands coming home that day.

The luckier women, the ones with a thousand blessings, were reunited with their husbands, but many husbands were sick, they had scars all over their bodies.

Like Cissé.

That was where he caught his illness.

In 1992 we had a boy, Ibrahim Cissé (see birth certificate).

He was our third child, but our first boy.

We already had two girls: Dalila, born in 1987 (see birth certificate), and Coumba, born in 1990 while Cissé was hiding in the garage (see birth certificate).

In all, we had six children (see birth certificates).

Alright, now back to work, I told him. There are thousands and thousands who are dead but you, you are still here. Light of my eyes. You must go to work.

So in the end he went back to work but he couldn't do a thing.

He was the boss but he had lost all his power.

The white Moors were the ones giving the orders.

Cissé had to bow his head and that's that.

It was unbearable for him.

Sometimes he refused to go to work.

Don't make trouble with the white Moors, I told him.

But he couldn't help it.

I am not your slave. I am nobler than you. If you want to kill me, go on and kill me, I don't care, but I will not walk behind you. Never, ever.

That is why we had to go into exile.

And also because Cissé was attending meetings, but I don't know what about exactly.

He didn't tell me anything, to keep me out of danger.

We chose France.

The land of human rights. Les droits de l'homme.

But it was hard for us to get a visa.

The French embassy doesn't give visas to people like us.

In the end it was his godfather who helped us.

He worked at the Spanish embassy in Mauritania.

We went to see him.

And we talked.

And talked and talked.

You can't take the children with you, if you do they'll see that you're trying to flee. Tell them you're going on vacation for a month and that's that.

We did as he said.

We left the children with friends in Senegal and then we fled, in 2005.

We passed through Tunisia, stop, then through Spain, stop, then we got to Paris and from there we took a train to Besançon, where my two brothers are.

I have two brothers who've been in Besançon for a long time. They are still there (see photocopy of electric bill and photocopy of rent statement).

We applied for asylum (see photocopy of temporary residence permit).

Papers, papers, papers, they were always demanding papers.

This was back before they started taking fingerprints, so we were allowed to apply for asylum in France even though we had passed through Spain.

But Cissé was tired.

He was too tired.

Exhausted.

One day, he would be fine.

The next day, no.

One day yes.

One day no.

We finally went to the hospital.

His illness had returned.

We were granted permits for sick foreigners that allowed us to stay in France (see enclosed photocopies of temporary residence authorizations issued by the Prefecture in March 2006).

But Cissé wanted to know the name of his illness.

He didn't want them to hide the truth from him.

They told him he had terminal cancer.

Sometimes he would fall asleep and the doctors would say it was over, and then he would wake up.

I spent all my time at the hospital.

I slept there.

Every day.

I knew all the nurses.

They even wanted to give me a job, I was there so much.

I was part of the scenery.

But one day Cissé said he wanted to go back to Mauritania, so he could die at home and see the children one last time.
I had filled out all the asylum paperwork, I almost had a job at the hospital, but he wanted to go home, it was his last wish.
So I ended up bringing him back home.
The nurse told me: We're here for you.
We'll give you an ambulance ride with all your luggage to Paris.
They even wanted to pay for our flight, but our tickets hadn't expired.
And so we returned to Nouakchott.
To Cissé's family.
It was hot there. This was in June.
The children came to meet us.
One morning, Cissé says to me all of a sudden: I'm going out to buy a cell phone.
What are you going to do with a cell phone?
Come on, I want a cell phone.
I said okay.
He wasn't supposed to go out.
It was not at all wise.
The white Moors knew he had applied for asylum in France.
Which meant he was against the regime.
A dissenter and all that.
But Cissé, he didn't care, he wanted his cell phone.
Toward the end he had strange thoughts, strange desires.

I couldn't tell him no.

He walked out into the street and right away they spotted him.

That night they came to see us.

The white Moors.

Mama, there are people at the door.

What do you want?

We want to have a chat with Cissé.

Just leave us alone.

There was a whole crowd outside.

They ended up leaving but they shouted insults on their way.

They spat on our door.

The white Moors.

We cried because it was happening again like before.

Cissé, you're going to leave me, I told him.

You're going to leave me and then I'll be all alone with this problem.

Two weeks later, he passed away.

June 26, 2006, at 9 a.m.

In our culture you grieve for four months and ten days, without leaving the house.

That is what I did.

And in the meantime my French residence permit expired.

I had waited too long.

I took the children to a safe place in Senegal because once again I was afraid of the white Moors.

Cursed days.

I didn't know where to go.

I hid, first in one house, then another.
I wanted to come back to France but I couldn't get a visa.
In 2012, at last, Cissé's friend, the same one, helped me.
He knew a person at the consulate.
We sold some land, we paid someone in an office, and at last I got a Schengen visa, six years later!
I took the same route as before.
Tunisia. Stop. Spain. Stop. Paris. Besançon.
Six years later.
I picked up where my husband and I had left off in 2006.
The Prefecture gave me an appointment on September 7, 2012.
They recognized me right away.
Mrs. Cissé, is that you? Where on earth have you been?
I brought my husband back to Mauritania, it was his last wish.
But weren't you in the middle of applying for asylum?
Yes, we had to stop everything.
And I showed them my passport.
And that's when they saw that I had come back through Spain.
This is a Schengen visa, they said. You'll have to go see about it with Spain.
What?
Yes, Spain.
I had to apply for asylum in Spain.
But I don't know Spain. I have nothing to do with that country.
I speak French.
They said I had been Dublined.
What? What does that mean?

I yelled and yelled.

No, that can't be! What am I supposed to do in Spain? I don't know anyone there. I've never even set foot there. Mauritania used to be part of FWA. French West Africa. I want to go to France.

No one listened to me.

I was talking to the flies.

One morning the police came for me at my brother's house. Luckily I wasn't there.

He called me right away: Hide, or else it's Spain.

I went to my other brother's house.

Stay here, Auntie.

I hid out for a week.

In the end they forgot to come for me.

So I prepared applications and applications and applications.

To not go to Spain.

The social worker, who was very nice, told me: Mrs. Cissé, you shouldn't have given them your passport with the visa, you shouldn't have told the truth, no one asked for the truth.

But I have the right to asylum wherever I want.

And the Prefecture knows me. I've already been there, six years ago.

I brought everything to the social worker's office: all the paperwork from my husband's illness, national health insurance card, hospital bills, chemotherapy, OFPRA receipt, all of it, all of it, all of it.

And we photocopied everything for the Prefecture.

Papers, papers, papers.

Envelopes this thick.

And we waited and waited some more.

Finally they allowed me to apply for asylum in France, but through the fast-track procedure.

You go to the OFPRA, and if the OFPRA says no, you go home. You can't appeal.

Even though Mauritania wasn't on the list of safe countries.

Even though I was eligible for normal asylum. It was just to punish me because I had refused to go to Spain.

So we wrote more letters and letters and letters so I could have the right to normal asylum.

And we waited, again, for months and months and months.

And the whole time I had no money.

I wasn't allowed to work.

I couldn't stay with my brother, there wasn't enough room.

I slept in a garage, I ate at soup kitchens.

Then, all of a sudden, one blessed morning, I received a certified letter.

All of a sudden I was no longer "fast-tracked."

All of a sudden I was entitled to everything, an allowance, housing.

My application for normal asylum was under review.

I went to the CADA to find housing.

But there was nothing in Besançon.

They placed me in Belfort.

I didn't know Belfort, but I couldn't refuse.

I moved there and I waited and waited and waited for the OFPRA's decision.

A thousand days I waited.

And finally I was granted asylum.

Normal asylum.

But now all of my children are in Senegal.

How am I supposed to see them again?

I have the right to bring my two minor children here, but they need passports, and Mauritania won't issue them, they say my children aren't Mauritanian, they say they should try Senegal, and Senegal won't either, on the grounds that they aren't Senegalese, and I just don't know what to do.

And my adult children?

They are still my children.

How am I supposed to see them besides over Skype?

How can I bring them to Belfort?

To where I live, on Rue de Madrid, in Belfort.

Because I live on Rue de Madrid!

Yes, really, Rue de Madrid.

In the end they still managed to put me in Spain.

Inshallah!

LOGIC
OQTF no. 66743

Given that Mrs. Tatiana Dakurgalia is Georgian.

Given that Mr. Jassi Guribedian is Armenian.

Given that their two children, Helen and Karan, born in Russia, are unregistered minors.

How does one enforce the law and expel this family from French territory, as mandated by the Prefecture and as further validated by the District Administrative Court and the Regional Administrative Court of Appeals, without tearing the family apart, when Georgia will not accept him and Armenia will not accept her?

MEANWHILE...

    the Eurasian cranes   *the skylarks*

         the bar-tailed godwits   *the starlings*

             the snow geese   *the white wagtails*

     the black storks   *the king quails*

       fly   *free*

       fly   *free*

       fly   *free*

        fly   *free*

        flee

LIFE EVENTS, FILE NO. 01126220022112

It was October 8, 2015.
They came for me around five in the morning.
They didn't ring the doorbell.
They banged on the door.
Very, very hard.
They banged so hard I had no choice but to go open up.
I think they would've broken the door if I hadn't.
I don't know how things are supposed to work here, but they didn't show me anything.
Nothing at all.
Not a single police document.
Grab whatever things you need, you're coming with us! You have an OQTF! Time to say goodbye to your family, you're a big boy now, you didn't want to go back to Kosovo all by yourself so now you're coming with us!
They were talking faster than fast.
It was very shitty.
They didn't have a translator with them.
It's because they knew I spoke French.

It was in my file.

I was no longer in the same file as my family because I had just turned eighteen.

My sister was a minor so she was allowed to stay in France.

My father had a residence permit for sick foreigners so he was allowed to stay.

My mother, since she's married to my father, was allowed to stay too.

I was the only one who wasn't, because I was an adult now.

There were a bunch of them at the door and three police cars parked outside.

They traumatized the whole building.

Because they actually handcuffed me to take me down the stairs to the car.

When I wasn't even putting up a fight.

My family didn't even react.

My little sister was there too.

She saw everything.

Would you like some coffee? my mother asked them.

We were so nice, it's sickening.

Can I see some proof that you're really police, that you're supposed to take me away?

They didn't answer me.

They just took me away.

I didn't even have time to grab my things.

Nothing at all.

They picked out my jacket, not me.

No, I don't want that one, it's cold out.//
It's that one or nothing.//
My father wanted to give me some money.//
Can I go to the bank to take out some cash?//
They said no.//
So I had nothing in my pockets.//
We went straight to the airport.//
Basel–Mulhouse–Freiburg.//
They had booked my flight in August, that's what it said on the ticket. They came for me in October.//
It was all planned out.//
Technically they were supposed to take me to a detention center first, but there I was, already on the plane.//
Between four soldiers and three police officers.//
It was very, very shitty.//
It was a commercial flight.//
Next to me there was this lady from Geneva, she shouted://
What right do you have to treat normal people like deer?//
Wait, like dogs, I mean. You say like dogs, right?//
I'm not authorized to speak to you, the police officer told her.//
And he shoved me into a seat, forced me to sit down.//
The lady was angry. Appalled.//
What has he done? What did he do? What did you do?//
I just turned eighteen and I don't have papers.//
She gave me fifty euros.//
That really helped get me through the first few nights back there.

I landed in Kosovo at 6 p.m.

The next day, my girlfriend texts me:

Hey! Wanna meet up this afternoon?

I hadn't told her about the OQTF, we hadn't been together very long.

I'm sorry but I can't meet up this afternoon. I'm in Kosovo.

What? I don't understand. Like you went home because you weren't happy in France?

No, the police came for me. I had an OQTF.

What's an OQTF? What did you do?

It's a deportation order. But don't worry, I'll come back. I can't stay here anyway. It's too dangerous. I'll come back.

And I came back three months later.

I took the same route as the first time, but this time it was a lot harder.

In 2013 there were so many of us that we walked right through the villages, the police couldn't arrest everyone.

But by 2016 Hungary had closed its doors.

There were police with dogs everywhere.

I was stuck in Serbia for four days. There weren't many people left to help you cross the border.

The fifth day, in a café, I met an Albanian who was planning a crossing.

Tomorrow night we're gonna try. If you want to come with us, come.

There were three Kurds and a Syrian, and me.

We got into a car.

We drove up to the top of the mountain.

Then we walked for a long time until we got to the Hungarian border.

In the dark, in the snow.

It was January.

Near the border the Albanian saw that there were police. We could hear the dogs barking.

You stay here, I'm gonna go see if there's another crossing point.

He never came back.

Later, much later, we heard the police dogs getting farther away.

We crossed over the border and then we ran.

We ran.

We ran for god knows how long without stopping.

I was so stressed out that I wasn't even tired.

I could have run all night.

I had a bag with a change of clothes so I wouldn't look like a migrant with mud on my pants, but I had nothing to drink and nothing to eat, there was no room in the bag.

We walked all night through sleeping villages.

In the morning we found a spot where there were taxis for Vienna.

Four hundred euros per person for a hundred twenty–mile ride.

The taxi drivers make round trips all night long, nonstop.

So they're exhausted.

The driver of the first taxi in line fell asleep at the wheel.
Right in front of me.
It was horrible.
I was in the second taxi.
I saw the car lying there with pieces everywhere, but we couldn't stop, it was too dangerous.
In Vienna I met up with a friend of my father's who drove me to Strasbourg.
At the French border, they were stopping all the cars to check passports because of a terrorist alert.
I got out of the car.
I'd heard they were letting people through on foot.
I walked right past them.
They didn't ask me anything.
And I went home to Besançon.
I filed another application for asylum.
I had a certificate from a doctor back in Kosovo saying I had been attacked there, by the same people as the first time.
The ones who loaned my father money so he could get treatment.
Guys who got very rich by lending money to other people.
I've run into them four times in my life.
They're scary.
They're violent.
Very rich and very violent.
We used to have a good life. My father was a chef. He owned a restaurant. My mother designed clothes.

We had everything.

But my father got sick.

To get treated, he had to borrow 30,000 euros from these people.

In Kosovo it's not like it is here.

In France my father got treatment for free. People helped us.

Back there you pay for everything.

The problem was my father kept getting sicker and sicker.

He couldn't repay the 30,000 euros plus interest.

1,000 euros a month in interest.

It had been three years since we'd borrowed the money.

We had to leave.

My parents and my sister went by plane, with visas for Liechtenstein. I went on foot because we didn't have enough money left to buy a fourth visa.

That was in 2013.

But when I got sent back to Kosovo in 2015 they found out right away that I was there,

the guys who had loaned money to my father,

Kosovo is tiny,

and they beat me up to get their money back but I didn't have any and they threatened to kill me.

That's what I told the OFPRA.

But it didn't help.

I filed an appeal with the CNDA.

But the judge says I never went back to Kosovo.

That I'm lying.

That it's not true.

But wasn't it the French police who came to take me away?

Not true, they tell me.

And the document they gave me at the border?

The document that says that on January 6, 2016 I left Kosovo for Serbia.

We know how things work where you're from. It's a fake.

And the new passport I got there?

It's a fake.

And the doctor's certificate saying I'd been beaten there?

Same. It's a fake.

And the photo of me on Facebook where you see me in my hometown, Prizren?

It's a fake.

That's absurd, I don't even know how to fake a Facebook photo.

I got another OQTF.

Now my last hope is a written procedure at the Besançon Administrative Court.

I have to put together documents showing why I should stay here.

Everything I've done in France up to now.

My report cards.

Do I get good grades.

Do I speak French well.

And on the other side the secretary general is putting together a case against me.

I already know what he'll say.

Everything you've done here, learning the language, going to school and all that, it benefits only you, it contributes nothing to French society, and you don't deserve to stay because you were rejected by the OFPRA and the CNDA.

The problem is they don't even open your file. They don't look. They have their answer already.

My lawyer asked the Prefecture for a document stating that I was deported to Kosovo by the French police, but we haven't been able to get it.

It is very, very shitty.

I went to the police,

who told me to ask the Prefecture,

who told me to ask the border police,

who told me to ask the Prefecture.

And now I can no longer file an appeal because they never answer. They do it on purpose, to stall.

Now it's too late.

So now I have to play dead.

It's the only solution.

Dead.

I can still go to school, they won't come arrest me on my way out of class

—I'm doing a vocational degree in catering at the Lycée Condé—

but I can't really sleep at home anymore, at night.

Because they come at dawn.
And they bang on the door.
Very, very hard.

MATHEMATICS

Given that it costs 20,000 euros to deport an undocumented foreigner from France* and that 21,000 undocumented foreigners were deported in 2013, calculate the total cost of deportations for the month of March 2013, using broader economic data to put your answer in perspective.

Solution

21,000 multiplied by 20,000 euros equals 420 million euros per year.

If we divide that figure by twelve, we get 35 million euros per month.

The French government spent 35 million euros on deportations in March 2013.

This figure is equivalent to the combined monthly wages of 14,000 people earning 2,500 euros per month (the gross average wage in 2013).

* *Estimates range from 12,000 to 27,000 euros per deportation depending on the source (the French government or the French NGO La Cimade) and on costs factored in.*

LIFE EVENTS, FILE NO. 45789999

I arrived in Paris on January 1, 2015.
I was just looking for a country where I could live.
Start to live.
Without religion.
Before I came here, I knew France only by name.
Nothing more.
I left my country, Afghanistan, in July 2014.
It took me six months to get to Paris.
I passed through all the countries along the way.
First I stayed for a few months in Iran.
Then I went to Turkey, to Istanbul.
In each country, I had to pay to cross the border.
Then I took a boat to Greece.
It's extremely dangerous, the current is very strong.
But you have to choose:
Stay where you are and suffer.
Or go to another country but maybe die on the way.
Maybe fall into the water.
You have to decide.

Yes or no.

I decided to take the risk.

There were thirty-six of us on a thirty-foot boat.

All night we were on the water.

All night in the darkness.

We arrived at five in the morning.

The boat was worn out.

Water was getting in.

The children were crying loudly.

Thankfully we got there in time.

Then I spent three months in Greece, in Athens.

That was the worst.

The police had given me a document so I could stay for thirty days.

After that, they captured me and put me in prison for a week.

Then they released me.

Then they put me back in prison.

I tried to stow away in trucks.

I tried to stow away on boats.

In trucks on boats.

I was captured several times by the police.

I was kicked.

Punched.

They hit hard.

One day, I made it across.

In a kiwi truck.

I moved the crates of fruit and hid behind them.

Thirty-eight hours I stayed locked inside that truck.

Thirty-eight hours.

Every half hour they turned on the cooler.

There were two of us among the kiwis, but the other guy went to Finland.

The truck was parked on a boat.

Then suddenly it started moving: we had arrived in Italy!

I knocked on the side of the truck,

taptaptap, very hard,

because we wanted to come out, we hadn't eaten anything, it was too cold, but the driver didn't hear us.

Then he made a stop to get gas.

I clacked with a key I had in my pocket,

taptaptap, very very very hard

and he opened the door and found us.

The police came.

I was not well at all.

They took me to the hospital.

Then they gave me a piece of paper.

You have twelve days to decide before you fill out your application for asylum, twelve days to see if you like it here or not.

I took a train to Rome. I stayed for fifteen days.

I decided not to apply for asylum in Italy. I didn't give them my fingerprints. I left.

I went to Milan.

Then I bought a train ticket to Nice.

Then another train to another city, I don't remember which one, it was two hours from Nice, maybe Lyon? It was much colder than Italy, I didn't have a jacket, I stayed in the train station from midnight to 6 a.m., it was very windy, I was all alone, and all of a sudden four guys, some black and some white but from where I don't know, came up to me and asked me something in French.
I didn't know a word of French. Not even bonjour.
What do they want from me?
What's going on here?
Truly, I was afraid.
They were alcoholic people.
One of them touched my bag.
Another grabbed my hat.
Do you speak English?
I said no.
They tried to open my bag and reach into my pockets.
They shoved me.
Then they stole my hat.
I thought: maybe this is how my life ends?
Maybe this is death?
Afterwards, I managed to get away from them, to go to a different part of the station.
But I didn't sleep at all that night.
I walked.
I sat.

I walked.

I sat.

Until morning.

Then, as I was looking at the departure board to see which train was going to Paris, I saw some people who looked kind of like me and I thought maybe they spoke my language.

Hello? Where do you come from? I asked in English.

Afghanistan.

One of them spoke Pashto.

I'm going to Paris.

So are we.

I was a little relieved.

I wasn't alone anymore.

I explained about my night with the alcoholic people.

Want some tea? Coffee?

I had a hot coffee.

Then I took the train to the Gare de Lyon in Paris and when I arrived I called an Afghan who had been in Paris for a long time, a cousin of a cousin back in Afghanistan.

He was by the Gare de l'Est train station, playing soccer.

I'll come get you after the match.

Okay.

I looked for a place to wait in the sun.

I was frozen.

He took me to the park near the Gare de l'Est.

Here there are people who give out food and clothing. You'll also need a blanket because tonight you're sleeping outside.

What, there's no bed for me? No camps? No gymnasiums? I was truly surprised.

This wasn't how I thought France would be.

How am I supposed to sleep outside in the cold?

You layer your clothes. Even if they're dirty, it's okay, it's to protect yourself.

Otherwise you'll get sick or even dead.

I did as he said.

I found a blanket and some clothes.

Right next to the Gare de l'Est, there's a place where you can sleep under the archway of a building. Under people's apartments.

A lot of Afghans used to sleep there.

Now they've blocked it off with metal fences. You can't go there anymore.

I ran into three people there who I had met in Istanbul.

Only in France did I have to sleep outside.

In Istanbul I was in an apartment for refugees.

In Greece too, there were beds for us. Three euros a day.

It's a whole industry.

In Italy there are big camps.

Only in Paris is there nothing.

There's no way I can stay here, I thought.

Then some Afghans told me:

There's a number. Every morning, you have to call 115 to request a bed for the night. You give your name and date of birth. Sometimes it works, but not always.

Once I had to sleep outside the Gare de l'Est.

When it opened, at the end of the night, I went into the waiting area to warm up.

I was tired and I wanted to charge my phone.

I slept for maybe ten minutes.

When I woke up, my bag was gone.

It's not so bad, I thought, I still have my phone and charger.

But after that I was really in trouble.

I had no clothes, nothing.

I had to start all over again.

At the 115 shelters there are showers, but it's dirty.

There are alcoholic people who pee on the beds.

I got sick there many times.

During the day, I would go to the library at the Centre Pompidou to be warm, to charge my phone, to use the internet, to read the news.

That went on for eight months.

Then I got a temporary residence permit and the France Terre d'Asile association gave me a room in a hotel near République. I started taking French classes because I didn't understand anything.

I enrolled at Français Langue d'Accueil.

I applied for asylum in France.

I was given a notebook to write my story and then in December 2015 I got an interview at the OFPRA.

I had to tell the story of why I left.

Every time I think of that story, it hurts.

Because back there ...
Back there ...
It still hurts.
Back there, if you don't accept the religion, you're an infidel.
In Afghanistan, 99 percent of people are Muslim.
Personally I don't like praying five times a day, but back there it's the law.
I'm Muslim, hamdulillah, but Islam, the way it is back there, I don't like it.
When I was little, the mullah hit me every day.
On my hands. On the bottoms of my feet.
Every day.
I went to Koranic school for four years and every day the mullah hit me with a wooden stick.
One day he hit me so hard on the bottoms of my feet that for three days I couldn't walk.
Every time I put my foot on the ground, tears fell from my eyes.
So I decided to stop going to the mosque, but of course I didn't tell my parents that.
I went out like I was going to the mosque, except I didn't go.
One day. Two days. Three days.
The mullah came to my house.
Why has your son stopped coming?
They hit me very very hard to punish me.
Then the Americans attacked Afghanistan, the Taliban left, and I started going to public school.
Normal school.

I was very happy.
There were girls and boys. Everyone went to school.
I went until I was fourteen.
Then I started working in a garage to learn how to repair cars.
It was hard working there, but I stayed strong.
It's not so bad, I thought, one day I'll grow up and I'll work for myself.
I had a friend who worked with the Americans. He was a cook for the soldiers.
He told me:
Christians, they're like this and like that.
Then he gave me a Bible, in Farsi.
I could understand everything. I was happy.
Because the Koran is written in Arabic.
So I couldn't understand anything when I was in Koranic school.
I don't speak Arabic.
I learned the words without understanding, like music.
But the problem was one day someone saw the Bible in the drawer at the garage.
What's that? You're not allowed to have that, it's the book of the infidels.
I'm Muslim, hamdulillah, I was just curious.
He told the mullah about it and that's when the trouble started.
The mullah wanted to have me beaten as an example to others.
The police came to my house to capture me, but thankfully I was at the garage.

When I found out, I went to an aunt's house to hide. By motorcycle.

An hour and a half away.

I stayed there. One day. Two days.

I waited for things to quiet down, but every day they came to my house. They looked everywhere for me. At checkpoints they checked every car.

I stayed there in hiding for five days.

If they capture me, they'll throw me in a hole, bury me up to here and throw stones at me. These are people who understand nothing, who never went to school. They listen to what the mullah says as though it is the truth.

I couldn't go home.

So my maternal uncle brought me some money and at three in the morning I left for Ghazni in a taxi, down the backroads.

There I found someone and paid them to take... what's the word... smuggle me across the border, and I went to Iran.

That's what I told the OFPRA.

In May 2016, I got a ten-year residence permit.

Then I signed up in a job placement assistance program.

Now I live in the 20th arrondissement. I have a room in a refugee center.

There's a shared kitchen, I have a job, I have a roof, I'm learning French.

Sometimes I call my mother.

At first, she had some troubles. The neighbors stopped saying hello to her.

But now it's okay.

The other day she told me about a friend of mine.

He went to school with me.

He was a dentist.

He died in an attack, with other people of the same ethnicity, the Hazaras.

He was my age.

He was a dentist in Kabul.

That's life there.

Afghanistan is a lost cause.

Why?

Because some Afghans understand nothing.

They don't think.

They don't want to understand.

They close their eyes and their ears.

They stay always on the same path.

OF HOSPITALITY
The Guest Bedroom

Everybody knows there are people drowning at sea,
kids sleeping under bridges,
violent and arbitrary arrests,
you just have to look around in Paris,
just turn on the TV,
but in a way, it's all still an abstraction.
Three hundred thousand people.
It's just a number.
Hard to put a face to it.
It's better than not knowing, but it's an abstract kind of knowledge.
Things take on meaning when you can put a face to them.
This is a democratic society.
We expect the relevant authorities to handle issues related to undocumented immigrants.
And yet it's clear that over the past few years the state hasn't been doing its part.
It's violating the conventions it signed.
It's going back on its word.

It's standing in the way of the regular people who are trying to pick up the slack.

There were high-profile trials in Calais and on the Italian border, of people fighting to provide for refugees' basic needs, without making a cent.

Average people.

I remember there was this old woman in Calais who was taking in people from the streets,

to her it seemed like the natural thing to do,

she was convicted of smuggling and sentenced harshly.

And so when you keep hearing these stories over and over, you finally say to yourself:

And you? What are you doing about it?

I'm not religious. I'm not talking about compassion.

I'd say it's more a question of fraternity. La fraternité.

We had already considered taking someone in because a cousin of mine is one of the few Westerners left in Damascus, she's a nun with the Jesuits, she works in a refugee camp and she'd alerted us to the possibility,

and so the idea was already floating around in our heads,

we had gone to two meetings organized by the Syrians to see if we could host someone,

and so that's where things stood,

when a friend of a friend of a friend of a friend,

a survivor of the Bataclan attack,

I think she was a senior executive, making a good living, but after the attacks she dropped everything and made it her mission to help unaccompanied minors, the kids sleeping outside, and so she does outreach in the 18th arrondissement, near Porte de la Chapelle, and wherever else they wind up in Paris, the Gare de l'Est, the abandoned tracks of the Petite Ceinture, she looks for minors—you have to start somewhere—and what she does is she finds them a totally informal housing arrangement within her friend network and takes care of the paperwork so they can see a judge as quickly as possible and get registered as minors so they'll be in the state's custody, and so, this one evening, she ended up with a massive influx of kids on her hands, ninety kids, just her on her own with these ninety kids and only three or four hosts, so she sent out a super urgent appeal to an extended circle of friends of friends of friends of friends, and I didn't know her, I'd never met her, and all of a sudden I get this message in my inbox: Any chance you have a spare bedroom for tonight? One night, a week, whatever, we'll take it.

We've got a spare bedroom, so we said okay.

And that evening a lady brought Issa over.

She'd been contacted by the same network, she'd taken him in for a week but she was divorced with joint custody and she needed the bedroom for her kids and whatnot, anyway, she didn't have room so she brought him to us.

He showed up with his bag.

He didn't speak any French.

Not a word.

He's Malian.

He speaks Soninke and Bambara.
Now he can string together a few words.
He came here without a passport.
Without identity papers.
Without a thing.
He had to hand over his passport to the smuggler, who sold it to someone else.
Anyway, in the African network they use the same papers for twenty people.
That's the racket.
I came up with my justification.
We're taking this guy in because he's on the street.
I'm no cop.
He says he's a minor, maybe he isn't, how should I know — in any case he's on the street, that much is true.
Not that I can't have an opinion on the matter, of course.
Judging by his appearance, he's probably a minor.
But then he's probably been prepped.
Meaning they told him not to carry papers, because he'd be better off that way.
They had him memorize a date of birth: April 20, 2001.
Is that the real date?
No idea. But it shows he's a minor.
And he clearly came here for economic reasons.
There's no war where he comes from, that's not the problem, but there's dire poverty, and so the elders in the village single

out three or four young boys and they pay for the trip, the smugglers, etc.

I've pieced together his journey bit by bit.

I've never asked him a single question.

His story is ultimately his alone, and a painful one.

But I do know they left in a truck, they crossed the desert, then they got to Libya, then the boat, then Italy.

The only thing he told me was that the boat stalled out.

For several days they were stranded there, at sea, with nothing to eat.

They were rescued by an Italian boat.

He didn't know how to swim, he'd never seen the sea.

It took him three months to get here.

He managed not to register as an asylum seeker in Italy, not to leave his prints there.

Which means he knew the traps to avoid.

It also means his trip had been carefully planned out in advance.

The village picked him over others to come here and be successful, on the grounds that he's a minor and he'll find a job.

And so his reality is that he's going to have to send half of his salary back to the village for X years to repay his debt.

That's what his life is going to be.

I don't know how they decide which kids to send.

What I do know is this wasn't some free and spontaneous decision on his part.

He didn't just wake up one morning and think:
Hey, why don't I cross the desert, the sea, risk my life?
He didn't have much of a choice.
He's from the Kayes region in western Mali, near the Mauritanian and Senegalese borders.
It's a very rural area.
You can tell he doesn't know the big city. He comes from the sticks, he never even set foot in Bamako.
I realized this when I took him on a walk around Paris.
I saw the city through his eyes and it was incredible.
Everything was larger than life.
Everything was new.
Everything.
The lights. The crowds. The cars. The ads.
He's never been to school.
There is no school in his village.
Well, there is one, but it's a Koranic school.
He didn't go there.
Maybe his father didn't want to enroll him, I don't know.
There's local resistance there, because those Koranic schools are totally alien.
In Mali, you'd think if anything they would have kept the French school system from the colonial era, but no.
Meanwhile, Saudi billionaires have put up these Koranic schools everywhere, with a hardline brand of Islam that's nothing like the pluralistic Islam they practice in Mali.
African Islam isn't the Islam of the Salafists.

So yes, there is resistance in the villages.

But there aren't any other schools.

Right now I'm giving him French and math lessons. We do addition tables. He's at a first-grade level. We play shopkeeper together. This costs X. You give me Y.

The extraordinary thing for me is watching him learn and begin to tap into a whole new world.

You have a front-row seat.

For instance, I took him to the Musée des Arts et Métiers.

Twice.

He was fascinated by what he saw.

The printing system, the first presses.

He's discovering things that we take for granted.

Things whose magic we've forgotten.

In the room with the measuring instruments, there's a mechanical model of the solar system from the seventeenth century.

An incredible piece of work with rotating gears, etc.

He said: It's beautiful!

And it's true, the object was beautiful, he just didn't know what it was.

So I explained the solar system to him:

That's the Sun and that's the Earth and you know the Earth revolves around the Sun.

Really?

Really.

And the Earth spins on its own axis too.

And so you explain planetary rotation, basically from scratch.

I don't know what he'd been taught before, but he was overcome with joy.
I don't know how much he'll remember either, but I do know that he's really lucky,
compared to the ones out on the street,
because he gets to see that the reality of the Western world isn't *just* the reality of survival.
Of how to find something to eat.
Of how to get a spot in a shelter.
Of how to work under the table in an underpaid job.
Because you can spend forty years of your life in France,
if you're an undocumented immigrant,
and live entirely under the radar, and that's awful because, again, the reality of the Western world isn't *just* that.
It's also the Musée des Arts et Métiers, it's also books, libraries, museums.
I say also but I should be saying above all.
That's the sad thing.
He's an incredibly sensitive boy.
We bought him some workbooks and at 10 p.m. he was still at it, writing out the letters of the alphabet with the thirst for knowledge of someone who's never been to school.
He wasn't doing it just to be the good little pupil,
better make a good impression for the judge,
no,
he was doing it with that pure, genuine excitement we all felt

when we were little.

That feeling of power you get when you decipher letters for the first time.

I remember that for months I would read everything I could get my hands on. It was extraordinary, like a whole new world. Same with writing.

But there are also harder parts.

I had been briefed by a Senegalese friend who'd had a very different experience.

His ticket here was a student grant, scholastic merit, school and more school. But, he explained to me, he'd also come from a very remote area of Casamance. His first few months in France had been tough, he told me, especially as far as praying was concerned.

He had to ask some of the old-timers at the shelter where he was staying how to do the five daily prayers.

That was a problem for him.

You have to find a quiet spot, all that.

But then the old-timers showed him texts from the Koran that say you're allowed to combine all five prayers into one.

So that's what he would do every evening in his room.

Five in one.

That's a huge change of routine for someone who's very religious.

He also told me:

I didn't understand how toilets worked here either, because

where I'm from, and this is another religious thing, we wash ourselves with water.

And so it took him forever to figure out how to use toilet paper, he didn't dare ask anyone, he was in deep shit,

so to speak,

and so he told me:

It would be best if you put a bucket of water next to the toilet.

Anyway, to get back to praying.

For Issa it's the only personal thing — it's a constant, something reassuring — he can take with him anywhere in the world.

Instilled in him at a very young age.

His prayer rug…

One day he tells me he's just come from the mosque.

I ask him which one.

He tells me: The one on Rue Jean-Pierre Timbaud.

That's where all the fundamentalists are. An unaccompanied minor going there? That's bad news.

We tried to warn him, but it wasn't getting through.

And that's when I realized that Bin Laden, the attacks, he'd never heard about any of it.

He was born in 2001.

I showed him photos of 9/11 on the internet, the towers collapsing,

he couldn't get over it, he was terrified.

Where he's from there's no TV.

One evening, we went to a friend's place to watch soccer.

Thirty seconds in, I realized it was the first time in his life he

had seen anything like it. He was physically reacting to the camera shots, the slow motion, the zooms. He was captivated.
He's been blessed by the gods, this boy.
So blessed that the judge,
unlike how it usually goes,
granted him minor status at his first hearing.
He got a spot in a shelter near the Place de Clichy.
He stayed with us for a month.
His application is moving along, he's in the custody of the state, he's housed, fed, laundered, he's got all that going for him, but even so, these kids, they don't really know what to do with themselves.
Where he's living they're all minors, and a lot of Malians.
He speaks Bambara all day, he's using his French a lot less, they just have two hours of class in the morning, that's all, in the afternoon they hang around, there's maybe a ping-pong table or something in the corner, a few outings, and that's about it.
When you're sixteen you need a lot more activity than that.
As for us, it would be dangerous to make ourselves known.
We advised him to delete all the contacts from his phone.
He's supposed to be an unaccompanied minor, so if they figure out he's got people here, that's bad news for him.
We see him from time to time on the sly.
But we steer clear of the shelter.
We were in Montreuil the other day. I told him:
Montreuil is Mali's second biggest city after Bamako.
I asked him if he had any cousins living there.

He said:

No.

That can't be, my Senegalese buddy told me.

He has to say he's an unaccompanied minor to improve his chances of getting his papers, but he's got to have a cousin, an uncle, a cousin of a cousin, a friend of a friend. See, my cousins, my Senegalese buddy told me, they're not my first cousins. My father, he had three wives, so between brothers and sisters, half-brothers and half-sisters, there are twenty of us, so just imagine the cousins, but he can't say anything about it so long as he doesn't have his papers.

The funny thing is,

even though his journey was successful in a way

— he made it, unlike some —

that was the easy part.

He's starting to realize what's in store for him here.

And contrary to what they told him in his village, it's no bed of roses.

It's a life of debt repayment through unskilled and thus poorly paid labor. A life in a shelter.

A bachelor's life, at that.

The golden age of immigration is over, the years when, even if it was hard, there was a family reunification policy.

Not anymore.

It's a lonely life, scraping by on odd jobs and little hustles, living hand to mouth.

Forty years of that.

And he can't just go back to his village if he fails.

That's out of the question.

Is he better off here than back there, I wouldn't know.

There's a big lie about life here.

A lie spread by immigrants.

It's a matter of pride.

The guy who returns to his village, even if he's a trash collector, he brings gifts for everyone, he's all decked out, he sends money every month, and obviously he's not going to talk about the other stuff.

He's the ambassador of the village, in a way.

Maybe it will be different for Issa?

That's why we're doing this, anyway, and why we're going to keep doing it.

It's a drop in the ocean, and there's something unfair and arbitrary about it too.

Why him and not someone else?

Well, he was the one entrusted to us. Simple as that.

PHILOSOPHY

Is the State the enemy of freedom?

Is the Nation a myth?

Does man make History or vice versa?

Is life fair?

To be happy, must one be indifferent to the world?

What's the point of philosophizing?

MEANWHILE...

                the wood pigeons   *the chimney swifts*

      the house sparrows

the swallows

        the Eurasian teals

            the rock doves

                              the spotted flycatchers

spread their wings   *and*

    fly   *free*

        fly   *free*

            fly   *free*

                fly   *free*

                            flee

LIFE EVENTS, FILE NO. 9878692438882

Look, I didn't want to come to France.
It's not that I don't like France, but I wanted to go to England.
Because of English.
It's easier to learn.
In Italy — this was in Rome —
the smuggler told us — we had come from Libya,
we had no idea about these things —
he told us:
For England, it's direct: 1,000 euros for the two of you and the three children.
But how does it work, we don't have passports?
Here in Europe they won't ask you for anything, just your train tickets.
Okay, I said, if it's as easy as that, then okay.
And I paid.
Except the train stopped in Milan.
It wasn't direct.
There was another one across from us. We got on.
We were barely ourselves.

We were scared of everything after Libya.
We rode for a long time and then we arrived in Dijon.
Everyone got off.
We didn't know Dijon.
Where is that?
In England?
We knew nothing about it.
The conductor asks us what we're doing there.
We bought tickets for England, I tell him in English.
He laughed:
This is the last stop. Everybody off!
That's how we ended up in Dijon.
In June of 2011.
We had left our country in 2006, my wife and I.
We come from a region of Ethiopia called Oromia.
My wife and I, we've known each other since we were little.
We had to leave because of the OLF — it's a group that defends the rights of Oromos.
I was a member, my job was to raise money.
I would go to meetings, at night, in secret, all that.
One night, February 8, 2005, I was asleep.
Soldiers came into my house, they put a pistol in my mouth.
Like this.
I thought I was going to die.
Thankfully my wife had gone to visit her family, she wasn't there.
After that, they put me in prison.

My wife had to hide in a shack outside of the village the whole time I was in prison.

For ten months she hid in that shack.

In prison they wanted me to tell them who worked for the group.

To name names.

Every night they came for me.

They put me upside down and splashed cold water on me.

They beat me with clubs.

But I didn't say anything.

By the end, they would come just once a week.

And then not at all.

But I didn't know how I was going to get out of that prison.

One day a soldier came to get me in my cell.

To kill me, I thought.

But actually it was to set me free.

Someone had given him money to do it.

A friend I had worked with.

That's how it is in my country. Corruption everywhere.

I went to meet my wife in Gomma and we left the country right away, we couldn't risk getting caught.

First we made it to Sudan.

Khartoum.

We gave money to a smuggler there to get us to Tripoli.

700 dollars each.

A 4x4 showed up.

There were thirty-two of us in that 4x4.

Held in with a rope so we wouldn't fall out into the sand.
We crossed the desert all the way to the Libyan border.
And there they sold us to another smuggler.
The smuggler who works Libya.
We had already given them 700–700 and now they wanted another 300–300 to get us into Libya and if you said:
I already paid to go all the way to Tripoli,
the reply was they hit you.
And not a slap like this.
They break your arm and there's no doctor.
They hit women too.
They step on their stomachs with their heavy shoes.
They crush your head while you're talking on the phone with your family and you cry out: Please, please, I'm going to die!
And the family pays.
They sell their land, their house and everything.
There were people with us who had been hit very hard, people who had stopped moving.
And so we were stuck.
Stuck in the desert with others like us.
Sudanese, Ethiopians.
Two 4x4s and a big truck full of Sudanese.
When it was time to leave
— everyone had found the money to pay for the trip, I had called the family, all that —
the Sudanese truck wouldn't start.
We had nothing left to eat, nothing left to drink.

We had to wait five days for the Libyan smugglers to come fix the engine.

Five days with nothing.

This was January.

At night it's very, very cold in the desert.

Very, very hot in the daytime, very, very cold at night.

We covered ourselves in sand to sleep, like this.

Out there, in the desert, you walk a few hundred feet and you find bones.

You go off to pee and you find skulls, teeth.

When the smugglers came back, they didn't even give us anything to eat.

They ate in front of us.

Like this.

We left for a town called Kufra, not far from Chad.

And again they put us in a house.

A big farm.

There were already four hundred people inside.

We found some water, a little food.

A baguette for two people with some Laughing Cow cheese.

And then they brought us straight to the phone for the money.

Okay.

200–200.

Okay.

To keep going.

To make it to Benghazi.

Otherwise they leave you to die in the desert.

Or they throw you in prison.

And no one can get you out of there.

That's how it is in that country, the smugglers are protected by the government.

They always have a father or a brother who's a general or a policeman.

Kufra–Benghazi is almost 450 miles.

But right before Benghazi, there's a little town, a suburb, called Jardinah.

Normally from Jardinah to Benghazi is two dinars.

But the smugglers wanted another 100 dollars per person, on top of what we had already paid.

They locked us in a big barn.

I saw things written on the walls, in my language:

Benghazi's not that far. You can make it on foot. You can escape.

That was written on the wall.

So I said to my wife:

Listen, let's try.

You're crazy. If they catch us, they'll kill us.

There's no other choice, I told her, we're out of money and we've already asked the family for too much.

Let's call my cousin.

My wife has a cousin in California.

Same for me, my father's brother lives there.

Oh no. If we start calling America, they'll just ask us for more and more money.

We can't let them see those phone numbers.

They were written on a piece of paper hidden in the belt of my pants, we had resewn the seam over it, like this.

So what do we do now? What do we do?

We talked to the others.

Some of them, it was their third time trying to cross.

Their third time.

One Sudanese, it was his fourth time!

They had been caught at sea.

They had been sent back to Kufra because they didn't have the money to pay the smugglers.

Next to me there was an Ethiopian whose leg was broken, completely broken, from top to bottom:

You see, I tried to escape, they caught me, they ran over me with a car, now I can't walk anymore.

So I thought:

There's no way to go back.

There's no way to go forward.

The only way is to call the family.

One more time.

One last time, just this one last time.

Did you make it?

Well no, but this is the last time. We need another 200 dollars to get to Benghazi.

The family sent the money and we got out of the barn, but we had nothing left.

In Benghazi, we had nothing left.

In Libya there are no asylum seekers.
You can't walk down the street like you can here, freely.
If the police catch you, they put you in prison and to get out you have to pay again.
Pay the police.
Luckily for us, we didn't get caught.
We looked for work.
I found a job in construction, but in Libya there are no contracts.
You work for one week and maybe they pay you for three days, maybe not at all.
The only people who work there are the foreigners.
The Libyans themselves are smugglers, they sell drugs, they rape women, they get into fights, all the kids smoke.
Even now, when someone mentions Libya to me, my body trembles on the inside.
We stayed in Benghazi for four months.
We lived with fifteen people in two bedrooms, men, women, all together.
We had forgotten that we were men and women.
We had just enough money for food and a bed.
But never enough to go any farther.
Never enough to get to Tripoli.
Finally, we decided to call the family in America one more time.
We told them the whole Libya story.
And they understood.

They sent us the money for the trip.

Benghazi–Tripoli: 400–400.

By bus it's not even twenty dollars.

We rode in a shipping container full of tomatoes, fifty of us locked inside, standing between the crates.

Under the sun.

And if you have to pee, if you have to throw up, you do it standing up, no way to sit down. Like sheep.

Yes, like sheep.

My wife was pregnant.

We told the smugglers we wanted to go to Europe.

Where in Europe?

Italy.

1,200–1,200. It's a big boat, brand new. It has a GPS. It has everything.

Okay.

So they brought us to the seashore, but then we waited a week for enough people to fill the boat.

Finally, they hadn't found enough people, so what do they do?

They come with a little boat, like this.

Like the ones you see on the Doubs.

It was no heavier than a table.

I know because we carried it out to the water ourselves.

Then my wife said: I don't have a good feeling about this.

She said: I'm scared.

She said: We might die.

Come now, what are you talking about?

She said: I had a dream. We don't make it to Italy. We never make it.

She said: They won't even find our bones.

But we already paid, what else are we supposed to do?

We got into the boat.

There were twenty-eight of us.

That's when I discovered the scam: the GPS was dead.

The driver had never touched a boat.

He was an Algerian.

We left at 4 a.m.

All day. All night. All day. All night.

Four days like this.

On the fifth day, off in the distance, I saw the lights of a big boat.

They can help us, I told the driver. Go! Go!

No no, that's Malta.

Malta is Europe, come on, let's go.

No way, I'm Algerian, they don't take Algerians in Malta, they'll deport me, we're going to Italy. Tomorrow we'll be in Italy.

And everyone in the boat: We're going to Italy, we're going to Italy!

On the sixth day, we were still at sea.

We had nothing left to eat, nothing left to drink.

There was vomit everywhere in the boat.

On the seventh day, I found a man, an Eritrean, like this.

Deceased, dead.

I said:

Guys, we didn't save this man by going to Malta, and now we have no other choice but to throw him into the sea.

The next day we found two other people, same thing. A lady and a little boy.

It started raining.

We held our life jackets out, like this, to drink the water.

One guy started eating Colgate. Toothpaste.

Every night more people stopped moving, went stiff.

And then the captain, the Algerian, he died too.

I tried to start the engine but the cord broke. It came off in my hand.

Now there's no hope, I said.

Except the wind.

The wind that carries us here and there.

Water started getting into the boat.

I tried to remove it, like this, with my hands.

Then a Sudanese said: There's a boat.

He had lost his mind.

He said: I'm going to go get the boat.

There is no boat, what are you talking about, stay here.

He said: Yes there is, yes there is, look!

He swam away.

In the end, there were ten of us left in the boat.

Out of twenty-eight.

My wife was sitting on the edge.

She had stopped talking. She had stopped moving.
Except her eyes.
Except her heart, her heart still going.
We spent thirteen days like this.
We couldn't even lift the bodies to throw them overboard.
We were too tired.
A strong wind rose up.
It pushed us along.
Then off in the distance I saw a fishing boat, with those things you use to catch fish. A Libyan boat.
Okay, we're saved, this is it.
There were only seven of us left.
Seven people.
Two women and five men.
The fishermen brought us onto their boat, onto the deck.
They took the engine from our boat.
They took everything.
Gold, wedding rings, my wife's earrings, everything.
And then they left us on the shore.
And they called the police.
Who brought us first to the hospital,
where my wife lost her baby,
and then, a week later, they put us in prison.
We spent eight months in prison, my wife and I, without seeing one another.
We got out in 2007.

It was a year since we'd left home.

In court, we had to sign a document saying we would never go to sea again.

That we would never go to Italy again.

We signed and were allowed to go free.

But what do we do now? What do we do?

We stay here. That's all. And we look for work.

So we can leave again later.

My wife found work, at a doctor's house.

Housework.

He had studied in England.

He had a bit of decency, human decency.

He paid her 100 dollars a month.

That was good.

Except my wife got pregnant again.

I went to see the doctor.

Give us some medicine. We can't keep this baby.

He said no.

My wife gave birth at home, without a doctor.

May 10, 2008.

A daughter.

My daughter: Bifitu.

She's in fourth grade now.

Anyway, I took over for my wife at the doctor's house.

Washing the rugs.

Washing the cars.

All day on my feet.

The clinic.

The garden.

We tried to leave again.

We tried to go through Egypt.

Over there, it's a different system, there are no smugglers.

There are NGOs.

If you're lucky, you get chosen for an interview.

But we weren't chosen.

By misfortune, we weren't chosen.

Let's try by sea one more time, my wife said.

1,300–1,300.

We were at sea for four days, but the Libyan patrol boats caught us.

Back to prison.

Since I had signed the paper saying I wouldn't go back to sea, I thought: This is serious.

I changed my name.

I changed my nationality.

I said I was Somali.

If you have money you can get out of prison. If not, back to Kufra with you.

How much?

500 dollars each.

No no, I don't have that much.

I was talking to the police chief like this.

If you don't want to pay 500–500, it's back to Kufra and then you'll have to pay 2,000 just to get back here.

Okay, I'll pay 300–300.

Where are you from?

Somalia.

Deal. 300–300.

I called America again.

They sent me the money by Western Union and we got out of prison for the second time.

Look, let's stay here for now. We'll wait until Bifitu is old enough to leave.

That's what we did, we stayed.

But one day, later on, I come home and what do I see?

My wife in tears.

What is it now?

I'm pregnant again.

Oh no, I said, it can't be.

Go get some medicine. I'll swallow it and that will be that.

I went to the pharmacies but no one would give it to me.

So I thought: I need to find work, I need to make some money.

Every year in Tripoli there's an auto show with cars from all over the world.

I found a job with a German brand: Volkswagen.

Where are you from?

Somalia.

I didn't speak of Ethiopia anymore.

Okay. You can clean cars.

How much?

150 dollars a month.

I said: Great.

I told him that I had been in prison, all that, that my wife was pregnant, that I already had a little girl, all that.

Then why did you come to Libya?

I didn't know it was like this.

He was truly sad about what I was going through.

Listen. We'll put some money aside. You'll see. Don't say a word. To anyone. We'll figure it out.

He gave me money in secret, at night.

20 dinars plus 20 dinars plus 20 dinars.

It started adding up.

Little by little.

I said to myself, we'll be able to leave again one day soon.

But after six months my wife says:

How strange, look how big my belly is, how it's moving on both sides, look how strange.

I went to see the doctor we knew from before, the one my wife had worked for.

You studied in Europe. Please, sir. Could you examine my wife? If you want money, I'll give you some. I'll work for you, at night, during the day, whatever you want.

He had a little more decency than the others.

He examined my wife.

And it was as I thought.

It was just as I thought.

It was twins.

They were born on September 24, 2009.

Boona and Sabona.

It was a difficult birth.

They had to do a cesarean and all that.

Luckily the doctor was there.

I don't know what we would have done otherwise.

After that, with the three children, life became too hard in Libya.

I was working at the doctor's, in a restaurant, I was working all the time.

From 2009 to 2011, that's all I did.

Work.

In March 2011 there were protests in Libya, like in Egypt, like in Tunisia.

Anti-Gaddafi protests.

But it was bad for us.

It was bad for foreigners.

They started killing the blacks.

We couldn't stay there.

We looked for smugglers to take us by sea.

Everyone was trying to escape.

I called the family.

This time it's 300–300–300–300–300.

1,500 dollars, that's all, for the five of us.

That was the last time the family paid.

Our family in America.

We got on the boat.

There were two hundred and seventy of us.

The sea was beautiful. We were at sea for four days and we made it to Sicily.
From Sicily to Rome, we took a train.
Yes, a train.
There's a train on a ferry.
Then Rome. Then Milan. Then Dijon.
That's how we ended up in Dijon.
We were completely lost on the train station platform.
I didn't even know how to say bonjour.
Luckily, at the ticket counter, we found someone who spoke Arabic: he explained about the Prefecture, applying for asylum, everything we had to do.
Okay. We'll go there right away then.
At the Prefecture they gave us an appointment for the following month, and for a place to sleep they sent us to the CADA but when we got there they told us:
There's nothing tonight. Come back tomorrow.
What am I supposed to do with the twins?
They were two at the time.
I don't know what to tell you. You're not the only one. Come back tomorrow.
There were other asylum seekers like us waiting for a bed.
Somalis. Sudanese.
They brought us with them to Place Wilson, where there is a big park.
We slept on benches.
It was summer.

We could walk the streets freely.
It felt good.
In Libya they throw you out like dogs.
They hold their nose when they look at you because you're black.
The next day I went back to the CADA:
In a week you'll have a room in a hotel.
We went back to Place Wilson.
The others there were all kids who were on their own.
There were no families except for us.
They protected us, they took care of us, like the lioness with her cubs.
Shh, they're sleeping, they're sleeping.
Even some French people gave us food.
Out of solidarity.
And then we got the hotel room.
But that wasn't easy either: we weren't allowed to stay in the room during the day.
If the children break anything, you pay for it.
After 6 p.m. all we were allowed to do was sleep.
Not eat, not do anything, just sleep.
Two months later, they found a home that could take us in Châtillon-sur-Seine, a village fifty miles from Dijon.
I decided to learn French, fast, so I could explain my problem clearly.
There are volunteers there who give classes.
But life in the home was hard too.

Waiting.
That's all you do.
There's no cutoff date.
People sleep all day.
At night, they get noisy.
Because there's nothing to do.
You're not prisoners but you're not free either.
Every day:
Go check the mail.
And always nothing.
One year of this.
Then, all of a sudden, we get the summons.
This is my last chance, I thought. I can tell them all about my problem.
On my application I had written that I wanted to do the interview in Oromo, that's my native language. I speak Arabic, I understand English, but not well enough to make myself understood.
Anyway, I get there and that's when I find out the translator speaks Amharic.
Which is the official language of Ethiopia, but I speak Oromo, the second language. In my family we always spoke Oromo. I know some basic Amharic but that's it.
Please, Miss, look in my file. How am I supposed to explain my problem in that language?
We couldn't find anyone. If you don't do it today, it's an automatic rejection. Up to you.

My head nearly exploded.

Miss, since 1993, in my country, each region speaks its own language. I may not know France, I'm an asylum seeker, but I do know my country.

You don't decide, I do. This will be fine. All Ethiopians understand this language.

On the woman's face it was already a no.

I spoke for two hours in a language I only half understood.

My wife for an hour and a half.

We waited eight months for the answer.

And in the end, it was a no.

I filed an appeal with the CNDA.

Yes, true, you had problems over there, political problems, but it's been six years since you left Ethiopia, all of that is old now, the regime has changed, you're no longer in danger.

I got a no once again.

The regime has changed but things are still the same.

Corruption everywhere.

My wife got sick, from the stress.

We went to see several doctors, including a gynecologist who asked why she was like that. Mutilated.

Where we're from all women are like that, I said.

But you are aware that in France it's forbidden?

Really?

We explained this to the social worker handling our case.

Really? They do that in Ethiopia?

Well yes, 99 percent of women are circumcised where we're from.

So if your daughter goes back to Ethiopia, she'll be circumcised?

Well yes, obviously.

Are you sure?

Well yes. I know it hurts women, but where we're from you don't have a choice, that's the way it is.

We're going to file a new asylum application, for your minor daughter.

This time it will work, you'll see.

She was very happy.

We got an appointment at the OFPRA very quickly.

And one month later we got refugee status for my daughter.

Her, yes.

But us, no.

My wife and me, no.

We filed an appeal with the CNDA so we could get refugee status too.

We waited a year.

And in the end, we were rejected.

But they told us it didn't matter:

Because of our daughter we were out of danger, we couldn't be deported back to our country.

But we didn't have asylum either.

We didn't have anything.

Luckily, in 2014, there was a new law.

All of a sudden, thanks to our daughter, we were entitled to a ten-year residence permit, the twins too, but we had to come to the Prefecture in Dijon to show our passports.

And we didn't have passports.

And we had to come to the Prefecture in Dijon to show both our birth certificates.

And we didn't have those either.

In Ethiopia, 90 percent of people aren't registered.

So we had to do DNA tests to prove that we were the real parents of Bifitu and the twins.

And of course, we passed.

They were positive.

So now, we're good.

We're good.

The Ministry of Foreign Affairs made us birth certificates.

But on the forms, they mixed up my first name and last name.

So in our papers we are Mr. and Mrs. Zelalem, and the twins are Boona and Sabona Zelalem and my daughter is Bifitu Zelalem, even though it should really be Begashaw.

Zelalem is my first name.

But it was too complicated to change.

So now that's our name.

But we have the right to live here.

That's what really matters.

MEANWHILE...

the sparrowhawks
                   the chaffinches
                                         the cuckoos
            the bar-headed geese
       the Arctic terns
                            the bobolinks
                the snow geese
                the rufous hummingbirds
the woodcocks
         the knob-billed ducks
              the piping plovers
                          the ruby-throated hummingbirds
          the nightjars
     the emperor penguins
                   the albatrosses
            the whooper swans
            the olive-backed thrushes
                      the brent geese
             the sooty shearwaters

    the wallcreepers
            the white-throated dippers
            the peregrine falcons
the pipits
                the red-winged blackbirds
                    the grey-headed chickadees
                        the yellow-billed choughs
the song thrushes
        the pine warblers
                the whooping cranes
                        the yellowthroats
                  the blackcaps
    the red crossbills
                  the Bohemian waxwings
        the merlins   *the starlings*
            the white wagtails
    the hooded crows
        the passenger pigeons
                        the black redstarts
the grey herons

      fly   *free*

        fly   *free*

          flee

COMPOSITION

The following two interrogations, dated October 9, 2013, are taken from the minutes of an asylum-seeking couple's OFPRA interview. Use the questions to piece together the couple's story, then write a coherent account of the circumstances leading to their arrival in France.

1. Questions for the man
   First name?
   Last name?
   Nationality?
   Father's and mother's nationality?
   Ethnic or tribal affiliation?
   Religious affiliation?
   Date of birth?
   Place of birth?
   Place of residence?
   When did you leave for Russia?
   Are you married?
   What is your partner's ethnicity?

How many children do you have?
What is their nationality?
Were their births registered?
Do you have birth certificates?
Meaning?
Where are they?
Why did you leave Armenia on October 26, 2012?
When did you first have problems with them?
What happened that day?
Why did they need your land?
So what exactly did they do?
Where was your land located?
What did they do when you refused to give up your land?
How many of them were there?
Did you report the incident?
To whom?
What did the police do?
Did they log your report?
What happened to you after that?
Were you injured?
Where?
When?
How did they get hold of the police report?
Why a cemetery?
What cemetery?
What happened in the cemetery?
What papers?

Did you sign them?
What did they do to you after that?
Why did they keep harassing you after you signed the papers?
Were you hospitalized?
For how long?
Who took you to the hospital?
Do you remember waking up in the cemetery?
Did you encounter any other problems?
With whom?
How did they know you were at that hospital?
What happened at the hospital?
What exactly did this man want?
What did you do after the two days you spent in the hospital?
How did you plan your departure for Russia?
Do your problems have anything to do with your partner's Azeri ethnicity?
Did you encounter any other problems?
And your partner?
How did you meet your partner?
At what point did she tell you about her ethnic background?
Was your family accepting of your relationship?
Did you witness her altercation with your mother and the neighbors?
What incident?
When?
What were the circumstances of your partner's miscarriage?
Was she alone?

Where were you?
What did she tell you?
Where did she flee to?
How did you find your partner?
What was the exact date on which you found her?
What were you doing in Cyprus?
What was your residency status in the Russian Federation?
Did you apply for legal residency?
Through what channel?
Was it the same lawyer for both applications?
Were your applications successful?
Why?
Were your children enrolled in school?
Did you encounter any problems in the Russian Federation?
With whom?
Were they Russian?
Explain, please.
Was your partner with you?
Did you report the incident?
Why?
Was this the only time you were assaulted by skinheads?
Did you have any further problems with skinheads in the Russian Federation?
What happened in Adler?
What exactly did they do?
How did they find out about your partner's ethnicity?
Why the nurse?

Were you injured?
Why wasn't your partner with you?
Did you report the incident?
Why?
What do you think would happen if you returned to Armenia?
Whom or what are you afraid of?
How long did you stay in the Russian Federation?
On October 26, 2012, did you come directly to France?
When did you leave the Russian Federation?
What means of transport did you use to get to France from the Russian Federation?
Did you travel with valid papers?
Do you wish to add anything?
Do you have any documents to submit to us?

2. Questions for the woman
   First name?
   Last name?
   Nationality?
   Are your father and mother Armenian?
   Do you have a birth certificate?
   Did your maternal grandparents approve of your parents' marriage?
   What happened to your family during the events of 1988 and 1989?
   Did they encounter any problems?
   What was your mother's religion?

Did she speak Azeri?
Did she speak Azeri with her family?
What language did you use to communicate at home?
What can you tell me about Azeri culture?
Did your mother pass down to you any specific Azeri cultural characteristics?
Are you married?
What is your partner's ethnic background?
Do you have children?
What is their nationality?
Were their births registered by the Russian authorities?
Were they enrolled in school?
What were the circumstances surrounding both your parents' deaths?
Did you see their bodies?
When?
How did you know it was the Fedayeen?
What was the motive for their killing?
How did they find out about your mother's ethnic background?
Did you attend college?
What is your profession?
What were your reasons for leaving Armenia in 2002?
Difficult in what way?
What were the circumstances of your miscarriage?
How many months pregnant were you?
Who assaulted you?
Mainly the neighbors or mainly your partner's mother?

When did you meet your partner?
Did you tell him immediately about your ethnic background?
When did he ask you to marry him?
Had you met his parents prior to his marriage proposal?
When were you introduced to his parents?
When did they find out that you were Azeri?
What exactly did his mother say to you?
When?
Did you have any further problems with her?
Was your partner present?
Where was he?
Where did you go after this ultimatum?
Did your partner choose to go with you?
Where were you living?
In the same town?
Did you have any other problems with your partner's parents?
At what point did your partner's mother inform the landlord about your ethnicity?
How did she know where you lived?
At what point did the landlord ask you to leave?
Where did you go after that?
Did you have other problems?
When in 2002 was this?
Why did you go alone?
Why didn't your partner follow you?
When?
Where in the Russian Federation did you settle?

What were the circumstances of your reunion?
When?
What was your partner's reaction?
What was your residency status in the Russian Federation?
Your partner as well?
Did you go through the procedure to apply for legal residency?
When?
Did you file a new application after that rejection?
What was the result?
Did you go through the procedure to apply for Russian citizenship?
Did you encounter any problems in the Russian Federation? Explain.
How did these Armenians find out about your ethnic background?
How did the nurse find out?
Did you mention your background to her when your child was born?
When your partner's mother attacked you in Armenia, did you go to the police?
Did you go to the police in the Russian Federation?
Why?
Why didn't your partner report it?
What town did you and your parents live in?
What was the situation in Yerevan at that time?
Why didn't your parents leave, given the circumstances?
After your parents' deaths, where did you go?

What town did your paternal grandparents live in?
And where did your maternal grandparents live?
Why didn't your parents follow your grandparents there?
What do you think would happen if you returned to Armenia?
What are you afraid of?
What do you think would happen if you returned to the Russian Federation?
Aside from your problems with the Armenians in Russia, did you have any problems with the Russians?
Did your partner?
Did you come directly to France?
When did you leave the Russian Federation?
What means of transport did you use to get to France from Russia?
Was your fake passport in your real name?
Was there a photo of you in it?
Do you have this passport with you?
When did you have to give it back to the smuggler?
Do you wish to add anything?
Do you have any documents to submit to us?

OF HOSPITALITY
Mouthe

I'm the president of the committee but I used to be a police officer. I retired as a major over in Morteau.
One day in the summer of 2014 I was watching a news program on television.
There was some very violent footage of the fighting in Iraq, of ISIS, and it knocked me right out of my armchair.
Okay, I thought, it's all well and good to get upset, you know, but it would be better to do something!
Granted, that's a tall order when you're all alone out here in the Haut-Doubs.
I knew the French government had committed to take in 25,000 Christian families from the Middle East and I also knew
— since retiring, I've become a community advisor and president of the local tourism board —
I knew there was a big apartment available in Mouthe, in the building that used to house the mountain police division before it was transferred to Morteau.
Well now, I thought, maybe there's something to be done here.

I presented my plan at a district meeting.
Though I'd already run it by the district president to get his approval.
I'm pretty military-minded. I abide by the chain of command.
It's how I'm wired.
So at this meeting you have the mayors of all thirteen towns and the deputy mayors of all thirteen towns in the county, twenty-five of us in all,
and some were less than thrilled at the idea, even downright hostile, but overall the majority was in favor.
So I thought, all right, let's do this!
When I've got my mind set on something, I don't like waiting around.
I also knew I was going to have to set up a committee.
I contacted a couple of people I knew I could depend on.
I got the word around, put up flyers in local stores:
Meeting on such and such date at such and such time to discuss setting up a committee to host an Iraqi family in the region.
Nice and simple.
The meeting was open to public.
So when I see fifty people in the room
—because I had no idea whether there'd be two or three or fifty of us, this was totally uncharted territory—
I'm like, okay, what are we waiting for?
If we're all in agreement, let's get the committee running right away.

We set up an office and three days later I sent the paperwork off to the government gazette, and the ball was rolling.

I'd heard that the Ministry of the Interior had an office in Paris that dealt with Christians from the Middle East.

Commissioner Brot was the one in charge.

So I plowed right on ahead.

People never go knocking on the right door.

I picked up my phone and dialed Commissioner Brot's direct line at the Ministry.

I didn't know him. I kind of forced my way in, told the secretary who I was, I must have called three or four times before I finally got through to him.

He was delighted to have someone approach him about taking in a family. That's what he was there for.

But Mouthe? He was skeptical:

You know, sir, you're setting yourself up for a terrible ordeal. Your village is too small. You're in the middle of nowhere. Do you even realize how much work is going to fall on your shoulders?

Bottom line, he tried to talk me out of it.

But he put me on a waiting list anyway.

And then, unfortunately, there were all the incidents:

First Charlie Hebdo and the Hypercacher, then the Bataclan.

And France turned off the tap on visas altogether.

Everything went on hold at the national level.

Meanwhile, the district board had left us high and dry.

Because I'd gotten the OK for the big apartment.

We'd picked up the keys, furnished the bedrooms, the kitchen, fitted the place out with curtains, pots and pans, pillows, chairs, lightbulbs, rugs, and we were all set for January 1 just like I'd told Commissioner Brot, but weeks and months went by and we still didn't have our refugees, and on top of it I couldn't get hold of Brot, he was always in a meeting, it was a disaster.

We had a breakthrough pretty much by chance.

One day a lady from the area happened to mention to a Protestant association, in passing:

There are tons of refugees arriving each day in France, everything's ready in Mouthe but nothing's happening, at this rate it's all going to fall through with the district board!

And six months later, right in the dead of summer, this association,

which has a strong presence up in Paris,

ended up with a family of sixteen on their hands, coming from Qaraqosh.

Six of them were going to Ollières, in the South, but the others, they didn't know what to do with them. And then they remembered Mouthe.

Are you guys still interested?

So we held an emergency meeting and we said: Done!

We'd waited nine months, and within three weeks everything was settled.

And you bet we were ready.

Even the beds were made.

And so, on August 7, 2016, we took a couple of Red Cross vans down to the airport in Lyon to pick up our ten Iraqis:

Trezia and Hatem, the grandparents, Raad and Baraa, Wisam and Halah, and Saffanah, the parents, and Cristiano, Saha, and Tita, the kids.

All we knew was their names. We hadn't seen any pictures.

We'd made little signs in English: HADAYA FAMILY.

I'd also asked Dridri, a Tunisian national, to come with us.

I naively thought Arabic was the same everywhere, but it turns out they don't speak the same language in Iraq as they do in North Africa.

I saw right away that they didn't understand each other at all.

Luckily Raad spoke English — he was an English teacher back in Erbil — or else we'd never have managed.

At the airport, we met up with the association from Ollières, who had come to pick up the rest of the family, and then we all waited around with our signs, the plane was over two hours late.

We waited.

And waited and waited some more.

And when they finally made it to us, with their plastic bags full of holes,

just how you picture migrants, basically,

they were exhausted,

wiped out.

They'd been traveling for eighteen hours.

From Erbil.

They had a layover in Ankara.

But it was the day of the coup d'état in Turkey, poor things.

They'd been frisked.

They'd been pulled aside.

They were exhausted.

They were scared.

The grandmother, Trezia, had passed out back in Erbil, right as they were boarding, plop!

It was her first time on a plane, and leaving her country behind to boot, it was too much for her.

They slapped her awake and she finally got on the plane, but she was in a state of exhaustion like you wouldn't believe.

We'd spotted a little café where we could all have a drink together before going our separate ways, but the family said:

No. We'll say goodbye now while we still have it in us.

You'd think they were going off to the slaughter.

Everybody was crying.

And as for us, we didn't really know what to say or do, it was clear we were tearing a family in two, everybody was crying, even our own ladies.

It was heartbreaking.

So then we get to the vans, we'd managed to scare up a few car seats, but the old kind, what a pain in the butt those things were!

We all took turns trying to get the munchkins strapped in, we were sweating buckets, it was scorching hot that day, and these

Iraqi kids, they've never seen a seatbelt, they have no idea who we are, they don't understand our intentions, they're screaming and screaming, they just want their mothers to hold them. And that wasn't the end of our troubles, because then we had to drive back to Mouthe with a hairpin turn every few hundred feet, they were all half carsick in the van.

They were looking out at all the trees, all the green.

They'd come from Erbil, which is practically the desert.

So then we get to Mouthe and we have to walk up five flights of stairs to get to the apartment, and Grandma, she sits down on the second-floor landing and says:

I can't. I can't go any further.

If we have to carry her all the way up, I'm thinking, we're in trouble.

Thankfully, she mustered the strength to get back up.

We'd planned a little snack.

But they weren't hungry.

They were traumatized.

They just wanted to be left alone.

To just shut the door and rest.

Except there was this whole thing with the reporters.

Because they were in the loop, of course. Everyone in the area knew about it.

This junior reporter from *L'Est républicain* had told me:

The day it happens, do me a favor and tip me off. I'll get it on the front page.

So when we found out they were coming, I gave him a call.

He wanted to come to the airport with us.

Let them catch their breath, we'll see tomorrow.

So the next day, he shows up bright and early with his camera.

Then, one after another, they all show up.

TV crews, the whole nine yards. It was a big story, what with the recent terrorist attacks.

We were kind of wary about the whole thing, they didn't have papers yet, and given the ISIS business and everything, you never know, plus Raad didn't want his picture taken, he was afraid someone might recognize him, and on top of it all we didn't know how the locals would react.

Get a load of these Arabs, coming to gobble up our welfare.

No one said it out loud, but some were definitely thinking it.

Because I did get a few phone calls, at first.

From people who weren't happy.

I mean, that really gets me.

People here have it pretty good. They make a killing across the border in Switzerland, there are no foreigners out this way, no unemployment either, and they vote far-right, that really gets me.

Anyway.

So then we get started on the administrative formalities.

We'd already made an appointment with the OFFI bureau at the Prefecture.

The standard appointment to register as an asylum seeker.

And so, two days after their arrival, we took three cars and headed back down to Besançon.

Our appointment was at 8:30 a.m., which meant we had to leave Mouthe at 7 a.m. with everyone in tow, grandparents, kids, and all.

The car seats all over again.

The hairpin turns all over again.

We spent the whole day at the Prefecture. We even stayed past closing to finish the applications.

We headed back to Mouthe at 10 p.m.

It was the first time I'd ever seen a closed Prefecture with people inside.

There was an Iraqi interpreter on hand and everyone had to tell their story.

They want a story that holds up. They're sticklers.

Meanwhile, we were trying to decipher the documents.

They were all in Arabic. They were religious documents.

I had a list of specifications to follow to the letter.

It's my military side. Ask me for a sheet of four uncut passport photos and I'll give you a sheet of four uncut passport photos.

Raad had also done things methodically, he had a separate folder for each family member, documents, copies of diplomas, he had everything.

Not a single document was missing from their file.

Not one.

We did everything to the letter.

And a month later, it was all sorted out: they all had refugee status.

Whereas some migrants have to go back twenty times because they don't understand what's being asked of them.

Why don't they just set up a single window for all these migrants?

It's awful, they have to go the Prefecture, to the OFFI, to the CAF, to the social security office, and everywhere they go they're asked for the same documents. The same photos. The same papers.

That's French bureaucracy for you.

Now we're in talks to get another association near here to take Bara's family, Raad's in-laws.

Because she had to leave her whole family back there.

It's been hard on her.

On the whole women have a harder time integrating.

They're less involved in village life, they stay at home, it's their culture.

It's funny, really, but I get the impression it's harder now than it was at first for all of them.

The novelty has worn off.

They're homesick.

The kids are going to school, they're starting to speak French, the paperwork is done, they're settled in, but it's harder than it was in the beginning.

It's a kind of mourning period.

Plus, they've just found out their old house is gone.

It burned during the liberation of Qaraqosh.

ISIS blew up the whole city on their way out.

Raad showed me pictures.

I'll never forget them as long as I live.

The wrecked piano. The charred walls. The blown-out windows.

It was a nice house.

The grandfather was somebody important.

He worked for the Ministry of Agriculture.

And now he's lost everything.

We have to see about getting them a car, ASAP.

Because it's also hard always having to depend on others.

For instance, they go to church every Sunday, and mass here rotates around the region, from church to church.

So we need two cars to take them, every Sunday.

Fortunately, the parishioners have stepped up.

Everyone around here knows the Hadayas.

They're very observant.

It helps that they're Christian, that's for sure.

People here see them as folks like you and me.

I took care of all the formalities to get their driver's licenses exchanged.

Now we just have to wait.

And we still have to figure out what to do about the apartment.

Because it's a nice place, but it's on the fifth floor.

The stairs are rough on Trezia and Hatem.

There are plans to bring the rest of the family up here from Ollières.

When that happens, we'll move the grandparents to a more practical apartment on the ground floor.
Life is funny, things never go the way you'd expect.
We thought they'd all want to reunite in Ollières.
It's nice down there, they've got a big, single-story home, a former parsonage, and the weather is certainly warmer, but guess what?
They all want to come to Mouthe.
Yes, Mouthe.
They find it livelier here.

MEANWHILE...

The employees at the Prefecture inspect forms, ask for photocopies, demand originals, press a button to call the next number that flashes in red on the screen above their head, type on their computer keyboard, glance at the little clock in the righthand corner next to the battery icon, butcher foreign names, add items to lists, tick boxes, think about their supervisor, feel their legs go numb, go on a coffee break, read a text that says don't forget to pick up bread for tonight, roll their desk chair over the worn linoleum flooring, hand out temporary residence permits, ask questions, check passports, evaluate payslips, compare the passport photo to its original, write the last name on the first-name line of the form but how are they supposed to know the difference, think good thing they're here to do this thankless job, hang in there, just three hours to go, flip through paperwork, scrutinize signatures, squint at supporting documents, file certificates, repeat the same thing all day long and oh come on what language do they have to speak to these people, fidget impatiently in their chair, feel clammy in their armpits, stare down foreign faces, blank faces, tired faces, give up trying to communicate, after all, we can't take in all of the world's misery, meet quotas, stamp, staple, highlight, photocopy, shuffle, sort, file, hand off, note down, run late, run out of patience, what the hell time is it anyway, call the next number, close their eyes and escape to the seaside for just a second, let out an exasperated sigh, get a crick in their back, mix up two files, take a deep breath and carry on, start dragging but hey it's almost vacation, almost the end of the day, just one more hour till closing, that's right everyone, too late, goodbye, come back tomorrow, shake the blood back into their legs after spending all day in the same position, emerge through the sliding doors, make their way down the street, soak up the last rays of sunlight, board the commuter train, go home, go to sleep, wake up the next morning and do the same thing in reverse all the way back to the sliding doors, to the same chair behind the same desk, and so it goes, that's life, and there's already an endless line outside of the same people as yesterday or as last month and they turn on their desktop computer while looking at the framed school picture of a child and they call the first number that flashes in red on the digital screen above their head and they examine documents and they study faces and they ask for photocopies of the original and they ask for the original of the photocopies and they require translations and they tap at the letters on their keyboard and they fish for irregularities and they sniff out lies and they take their vitamin C to keep themselves going and they say good morning to their supervisor and they really hope they'll get that reassignment and they add items to lists and they fill in boxes and their knees are already bothering them, already, and they go on a smoke break in the designated smoking area where they read a text that says I love you, and they go back to their office chair and they try to sit up straight like the doctor said, better for the back, and they print out temporary residence permits and they cut along the dotted line around a passport photo and they look for a paperclip and they write the last name on the first-name line of the form, well why didn't you say something before, and they throw the defective form in the waste basket and they take a new one from a pile of blank forms and they start filling out the first line and then the second line and then the third line and then the fourth line, just six hours to go, and they think what a life, this isn't how I pictured it when I was little, and they look through papers and more papers and more papers and more papers to make papers, or refuse to make papers, and so on and so forth.

Today a new law, harrowing in its brutality, was passed in our country.
The tents multiplied along the canal, then, one sunny morning, were taken down, only to reappear.
One Armenian I had met was deported back to his country.
Another is still waiting for a response from the CNDA.
And a baby was born in Mouthe, to the Hadaya family.
His name is Lionel.

ACKNOWLEDGMENTS

I would like to extend my heartfelt gratitude to the people I met in Besançon, in Paris, and in Mouthe. They trusted me with their stories and their voices.

They opened my eyes.

I would also like to thank the French Collective for the Defense of Foreigners' Rights and Liberties in Besançon, especially Pierre Couchot.

The Français Langue d'Accueil association in Paris, Marysia Khalessi and Christian Robin.

The Accueil and Solidarité des Hauts du Doubs association: Gilles, Danielle, Denise, Denis, and Andrée.

My deepest thanks to the Hadaya family.

To Célie Pauthe, Marion Vallée, and everyone at the Centre Dramatique National de Besançon Franche-Comté.

To the students in the DEUST program, class of 2018, at the Université de Franche-Comté.

To Fanny Bernardin, Maya Guyot, Louna Loew, Juliette Mouteau, and Xénia Sartori.

To Quentin Schoëvaërt. To Michèle Constantini. To Philippe Grand.

And finally, to Pierre and Louise.